THE BOLERO OF ANDI ROWE

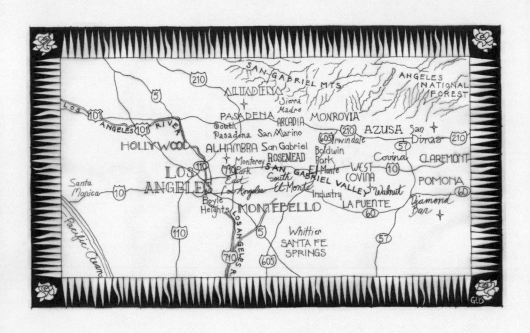

The Bolero of
ANDI ROWE

Stories

TONI MARGARITA PLUMMER

CURBSTONE BOOKS
NORTHWESTERN UNIVERSITY PRESS
EVANSTON, ILLINOIS

Curbstone Books
Northwestern University Press
www.nupress.northwestern.edu

San Gabriel Valley map by Greta L. Bilek

Printed in the United States of America

10 9 8 7 6 5 4 3 2 1

This is a work of fiction. Characters, places, and events are the product of the author's imagination or are used fictitiously and do not represent actual people, places, or events.

Library of Congress Cataloging-in-Publication Data
Plummer, Toni Margarita.
    The bolero of Andi Rowe : stories / Toni Margarita Plummer.
      p. cm.
    ISBN 978-0-8101-2767-8 (pbk. : alk. paper)
    I. Title.
PS3616.L876B65 2011
813'.6—dc22

                                                                    2010052518

♾ The paper used in this publication meets the minimum requirements of the American National Standard for Information Sciences—Permanence of Paper for Printed Library Materials, ANSI Z39.48-1992.

For my mother

CONTENTS

THE BOLERO OF ANDI ROWE

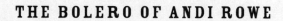

Yard Work

Rosa first steps out onto her lawn while Andi is rinsing the car. She stands very casually, taking in the street's activities as a whole, when she finally settles on Andi as her first item of business and begins funneling her gaze up their driveway.

Andi knows pretending she hasn't seen the old woman won't work. If Rosa wants to talk to her, she will just phone the house. She already has that morning, about the branches that have fallen from their palm tree and are littering the lawn and hanging precariously over the front porch. Mom's assurances to Rosa that she would tell the girls to be careful put Andi and Maura into hysterics, the intensity of which Mom only seemed to fan with the hushing, frantic waving of her free hand. They had their fun, but now Andi is being summoned. She should have known Rosa would have the last laugh.

Andi eases herself down from the car doorway, where she was standing to have a better reach drying the roof, flinging the towel lengthwise and slapping it over the car. She tosses the towel onto a plastic lawn chair, thinking she'll have to do the windows later, and proceeds down the long driveway toward Rosa's house, checking both sides of the street.

The house two down from Rosa's has been blaring the same waltz over and over, the music crystal clear, as if they have an orchestra in their living room. A bunch of high school kids practicing for a *quinceañera* are gathered on the overgrown lawn. The boys talk in a group, standing apart from the girls, until the director, a short woman wearing pants too small for her, screams, "Let's go! One, two, three. One, two, three," and then the boys jump into the girls' arms, grasping at their waists, an instantaneous forming of couples.

It's still morning. The ground isn't scorching yet, but it burns Andi's feet, and she breaks into a little jog to Rosa's lawn, where she is swallowed up by the shade of a tree. This is a tradition, Rosa "calling" her over like this, except Andi has never become comfortable with it and will sometimes actually avoid going outside when Rosa is standing there.

Rosa looks even older than Andi remembered, the deep crinkles around her eyes magnified by her big glasses. She wears a brown nylon scarf over her curlers. Andi wears a scarf, too—a pink cotton bandana she bought at a Bob Dylan concert in upstate New York. She went with a boy she kissed a lot there, but has not seen since. Between the two of them, there is no makeup except for Rosa's very red lipstick, which rides slightly over her top lip, making her look just a bit clownish.

"How nice of you to visit," Rosa says. She opens her arms, and Andi enters the hug hesitantly. Rosa has this way of hugging that makes it hard to breathe.

"You left the garage door open." Releasing her, Rosa nods toward Andi's peach-colored house across the street.

"I'll make sure to close it when I get back," Andi says.

Rosa knows that the pigeons like to stay in the rafters of their garage and that you have to chase them out by hitting the beams with a broom. If you don't, you'll just close the door on them, and they'll proceed to crap with reckless abandon. The pigeons are a perennial hassle, and their cooing sometimes embarrassingly fervent. When Sparkee, their last dog, was around, one might buoy in his water bowl like a rubber ducky. Too charitable or tired with age, he let them.

Rosa looks at Andi's chest. "And is that a school shirt?" she asks incredulously.

Andi follows Rosa's eyes. She is wearing a gym shirt from elementary school, navy blue with a yellow eagle. She found it in the closet and doesn't know whether it belonged to her or Maura, though that didn't stop her from claiming it. It is a little damp from where she got wet trying to turn off the hose, water spraying out from under the faucet.

"Uh, yeah. I just needed an old shirt."

"Well, it still fits you. I guess that's something! Will you have a seat?"

"Thank you."

Rosa sits on her bench under her tree. Andi sits beside her and adjusts her shorts. She did not plan on being out in public dressed in short shorts, a pink bandana, and a shirt she should have stopped wearing eight years ago. But Rosa is not someone you disappoint.

Rosa has lived in this house across from Andi and her family for as long as Andi can remember. It's hard to think that will be changing soon. Mom told them that Rosa's daughter finally convinced her to move to New Mexico, so Rosa could be closer to the family. Mom says that the daughter has been asking for years and years, and it wasn't until Tom, Rosa's husband, died, that she finally relented.

Andi searches the yard for signs of departure, but she can't find any. Mom has gone over more than once to help Rosa pack, always at Rosa's insistence, but she says they always end up moving things around, never actually taking anything out.

The houses in South El Monte all look more or less the same. There are variations in the placement and size of their windows, in the shape and depth of their porches. But mostly they are just one-story boxes with stucco slapped on. People *do* get creative with their lawns though, planting gardens, installing small fountains. One house down the block bizarrely features fake woodland creatures.

Truthfully, Rosa's yard is probably the nicest. Her grass is perfectly green and even. She has manicured hedges lining the driveway and the front of the house and a trellis of red flowers framing the small porch. A tree, big and plump like a mushroom, has white flowers blooming up high. Its low branches are thick and angular, like elbows, a sweet little birdhouse hanging from one. Around the tree are clusters of flowers, red and pink and white. A very low brick border, no higher than a foot, undulates around the corner of the yard. No palm branch or errant leaf would survive here for long.

But the best part is the bench, perfectly situated under the tree and giving a nice view of the street. Andi has only sat here a few times. No one else has a bench in their front yard. Maybe this is why no one else lingers. They set out sprinklers for their kids to run through, fetch their newspapers from the end of the driveway. They mostly leave all yard maintenance to the gardeners. But Rosa sits outside for hours at a time, keeping a watch on the neighborhood. If this were New York, she'd be one of those stoop ladies Andi is always passing.

"What are you up to this summer, *mija*?" Rosa asks her. "Do you have homework?"

"No." Andi smiles at the word. "But I'll have my final project this year."

"That sounds interesting. What is it?"

"We have to design a building or some kind of space that would fit in our hometown."

Andi feels anxious just thinking about her final year.

The rear of the car pokes out from behind the house, beckoning. Her ulterior motive in washing the car was to work on her tan. Each summer, she tries to get as dark as possible before returning to New York. She should be laying out right now, not sitting in the shade of Rosa's tree.

Rosa's strange silence isn't helping matters either. Usually by now Andi would have gathered some nuggets of gossip, like whose daughter got home drunk last night and who is leaving their lights on too much. But Rosa doesn't offer up any juicy tidbits. She just watches the quince-añera practice.

The kids now surround the *quince* and her *chambelán*. The boys take steps side-to-side, one arm behind their backs, the other out to twirl the girls who have it hardest and are spinning from one boy to another. They'll need to do it in heels on a dance floor but for now they're wearing tennis shoes and sandals, stumbling over the grass. The quince girl steps in front of the chambelán, and he puts his hands on her waist, tries to lift her off the ground. "Ow!" the girl yells and turns to give him a dirty look.

Rosa and Andi share a smile.

"I hear you're moving," Andi says, putting a chipper note in her voice. Maybe this is what Rosa wants to talk about and bringing it up will get her to her tanning session faster.

Rosa doesn't exclaim as expected. She adjusts a bobby pin and says, "We'll see."

"Oh, I thought my mom said that you were moving to New Mexico?" Perhaps she has heard wrong. But Mom talked about it as if it were all settled.

"Maybe. I haven't decided. *Pero, ¿quién sabe?*"

Who knows? Andi thought everyone knew.

A honking sound blares down the street. The *elote* man is rounding the corner, pushing his shopping cart, which is loaded with a tall plastic cooler of roasted corn, and in the upper seat, plastic jars of mayonnaise, chile, and salt. The quinceañera kids, ravenous from clumsily waltzing, leave their posts and descend on the man like locusts. He grins like a man who's struck it rich in Vegas, repeating their orders and calling out, "*¡Dos dólares, dos dólares!*" The kids are licking their fingers, laughing—it's one big love fest. Only the waltz director does not look happy.

"Yes, I haven't decided," Rosa says again.

The grain of the bench is cool and smooth beneath Andi's hand. It's oak, she realizes. She never would have known that before studying, but she can tell now.

"Are you moving back here after college?" Rosa asks, and she turns from the delicious scene of the director trying to shoo the elote man away to actually face Andi.

Coming back is the plan. Once she gets her degree, she'll move back in with Mom and look for jobs at architecture firms in Los Angeles. So she's not sure why she answers, "I don't know."

Rather than push for a more satisfactory answer, Rosa simply nods as if she understands and turns back to the street.

"Do you like this bench?" she asks Andi.

"It's really nice." She rubs the wood appreciatively. She can understand why Rosa likes to sit out here. She's even beginning to feel slightly envious.

"Tom made it," Rosa says, giving the bench a sideways look. "Did you know that?"

"Yeah, my mom told me."

Andi wants to ask if Rosa is taking the bench with her. Its fate seems important, even crucial. But Rosa doesn't seem to want to admit she herself is going anywhere, and Andi isn't sure what answer she hopes to hear. She says instead, "It's a beautiful bench."

"Tom said it would last forever. I told him, how am I supposed to know that?" Rosa gives a big shrug and folds her arms up into her chest. "I don't see how anyone can say something like that." Her shoulders are hunched up, and there's a scared look in her eyes. It's an unfamiliar picture.

"I think he was right," Andi says.

Rosa gives her a long look, like she wasn't expecting her to speak, and for a moment Andi holds her breath. Then Rosa faces forward and puts her hands on her knees. She nods her head and breathes out through her mouth.

Across the street, Maura steps out onto their porch, a little blond beacon. She is wearing the straw hat she bought at the bookstore at Pomona College, where she is studying anthropology. She bends at the waist, in slow motion, to dramatically tug on a palm branch.

Andi knows what she's trying to do. "I think I have to go," she blurts. "We have that situation, with the palm branches."

"All right, sweetheart," Rosa says, starting to sound more like herself. "You take care, and tell your momma to come by when she has a chance. I'd like to—" she falters. "I'd like to give her some things. *Unas cositas* for the house, *nada más*."

"I will," Andi says. Rosa pats her shoulder, but does not attempt to grab her again for another suffocating hug. Andi gives her a smile before running back across the street, her feet on fire those few steps. The waltz is starting up again.

"What was she going on about?" Maura asks, exasperated, like she was the one caught in one of the infamous Rosa tractor beams. She missed some spots at the beach yesterday so the backs of her arms and neck are a bright pink, shiny because they are slathered in aloe vera. Her tan manifests itself in freckles on her upper arms and nose. "Mom said I had to come save you. You owe me."

"Yeah, big time," Andi says. She looks back to Rosa, who stands slowly from the bench, places her hand on her tree a little absently, and goes back inside her house, smoothing her hedges on the way.

"Well," Maura says, eyeing the yard. "Are we gonna do this, or what?"

Maura goes for the branches at the edge of the lawn. Andi stands on the balls of her feet and pulls down the ones that are hanging over the porch. She handles them as lightly as she can—they have thorns along the edges, and, unsurprisingly, pigeon shit stains. A few other neighbors have short palms. But theirs is very tall and lean. When the wind and sun hit it just right, the branches move like they are under water, their edges shiny and waving like tinsel. The palms that fall are never like the ones still attached to the tree. These on the ground and roof are brown, dry husks, the shape of mermaid tails, thick and curving with little strips peeling off.

Maura is wearing sandals, so she's the one who plants her foot on the middle of each branch, pulling on the tail end until it snaps with a satisfying crack. As she's cracking them, Andi stacks the folded palms beside the rosebushes, where they will wait until trash day.

"Lunch should be ready," Maura says, heading back inside.

"I'll be right in," Andi says, already walking around the house to the backyard. She grabs a broom leaning on the stucco wall and evicts two pigeons from the garage before pulling down the door.

Inside, the kitchen is warm, but the ceiling fan sends cool waves of air down onto her shoulders. They are pink, a tan planted to bloom.

Olivia's Roses

All the flowers had put Olivia in a romantic mood.

It was her first time at the Tournament of Roses Parade in Pasadena. She'd only ever watched it on TV, and from that vantage point, sitting on the brown shag carpet of the living room, seeing it play out on the grainy, small screen, it seemed not romantic at all. More like a windup toy that never stopped, an endless stream of marching bands, floats, and men and women on horses. The announcers talked about the staggering numbers of flowers, the gorgeous weather, the legacies of whatever Southern California civic society. These were all details Olivia would forget a minute later. But now, in the bright, cold sunshine of the first day of 1970, with people pressing her on all sides, trumpets blaring, and a constant rumble beneath her feet, she had that feeling she'd get whenever Sister Bernadette and the other sisters from school took them to Disneyland, with its Sleeping Beauty castle and carousel and submarines, so different from her small world of school and home and not much else. It was the feeling that love was nearby, an invisible force field. And if she could only find it, it would lead her to another world. A world where girls glowed and sighed and wept. Where girls could act foolishly, even meanly, ignoring family obligations and moral codes.

Where they could scream at the top of their lungs and be forgiven everything. Olivia dreamed of living in that world, and, as far as she could tell, falling in love was the only way to get there.

Last week, she and Pandi had gone with the group from church to be petal pushers. They were given metal tools with a hole to slide over the rose stems, breaking off any leaves and thorns. With little razors they cut the stems to a dictated size and stuck the flowers into vials of water, finally pushing the vials into a chunk of Styrofoam that would be carried off when full. The year before, they'd had the job of filling all the vials with water. It was cold, monotonous work. Olivia was glad they'd been able to handle the flowers this time. She'd even kept track of all the colors they got: yellow, pink, gold, orange, and yellow tipped with red.

This morning at the parade, she and Pandi had been trying to guess where their flowers were. They hadn't been told which float they were for when they were helping. Olivia guessed it was a silly game. Their flowers probably weren't even whole anymore, cut up into pieces and glued onto any number of floats.

A float of a giant garden went by. Women dressed like butterflies smiled and waved.

"How dumb to make a float of flowers," Pandi said. They hadn't been there two hours and she was already complaining.

"But you can't see the flowers in the other floats. They're what make up the other things, the bigger pictures," Olivia insisted, savoring the carnation plumage of a huge parrot.

"It still seems weird to me," pouted the barely fifteen-year-old Pandi, and she stood on tiptoe to look at the crowd, more interested in the people.

Olivia didn't respond. She wasn't going to let Pandi ruin this. Abuelita never let them go anywhere, and she had only let them come this time as a reward for volunteering for the church, and because their brother was there. She had let him spend the night on the street with his friends, but Olivia and Pandi had had to get up while it was still dark and take the bus from Rosemead. Orlando hadn't been where he said he'd be either, and they'd had to search for an hour before they spotted him.

"Hey, Ollie." It was Orlando tapping her shoulder.

The crowd had her pinned at the shoulders, and she could only turn her head to see his chin. He had already passed her up in height.

A pungent, musky scent accompanied him. "You smell funny," she told him.

"Right," he said, laughing a little. "Ollie, I want you to meet my friend."

"Hi, I'm Anthony." A lanky boy with wire-rimmed glasses, blue eyes, and brown hair maneuvered himself to her side.

Orlando pinched her on the arm and whispered in her ear, "A él le gustas." He was gone before she could react.

Pandi glanced over at Anthony and took Olivia by the arm. They often stood this way, or hooked arms walking home from school. They were both wearing their miniskirts, forbidden clothing they'd bought in the garment district downtown. They'd wiggled out of their longer skirts once they were out of sight of the house and stuffed them in their backpacks. It wasn't such a good idea considering the temperature, but they'd already decided they were going to do this. Today was a special occasion.

"So how do you like the parade?" Anthony asked Olivia.

"It's pretty."

Pandi stuck her head of long brown hair between them. "Do you like my sister? Do you think *she's* pretty?"

"Pandi!" Olivia tried to squirm away, but the effort was useless.

Before Pandi could say anything else embarrassing, one of the guys behind them yelled, "Hey, Pandi! Your brother's smoking."

"What!" Pandi threw her arms over her head, hitting Olivia in the process, and twisted to get to their brother. The space she left was quickly filled, and the crowd pushed Olivia up beside Anthony.

"That was Pandi," she said.

"Pandi," he said. "That's different."

"It's short for Paulina. And my name is Olivia." Her grandmother had taught her to be polite.

"Have you seen this before?" he asked, motioning to the parade.

"It's my first time," she said. "And you?"

He squinted at the sun. "Nah. So what's your favorite flower? Let me guess. Roses."

"I like roses. We have some at our house. But I've never seen so many different colors before."

"You know that color doesn't really exist? It's just the way our eyes take in the light."

Olivia had a vague recollection of having heard something like this. Maybe in a science magazine she'd borrowed from her friend Lulu. She liked reading about plants, but sometimes she glanced at the other articles. She watched the floats passing. You couldn't see the flowers from where they were standing. All you could see were the colors. She remembered the bunches of roses she'd handled. Carts and carts of them. Yellow roses, red roses. She couldn't think of them as otherwise. And she didn't want to. They were beautiful. Was being beautiful a good enough reason to believe in something?

"Are you in high school?" Anthony asked her.

"I graduate this year."

"You going to college?"

She was caught off guard by the question. Usually people just said congratulations. "No."

"Why not? I bet you're smart enough."

"I have to work." The answer seemed obvious enough. She'd never entertained the idea of college for long. Abuelita had always written it off. It was assumed Orlando would go, but not her or Pandi.

He nodded. "I'm in college, but it's the pits. All that studying. There are other things to do. And I'd rather read what I want. What do you like to read?"

No one had ever asked her that before. No one that wasn't a teacher. The question sounded very different coming from him. "I don't know . . ."

"Hey, Tony! Look!" One of the guys had set off firecrackers in a trash can.

"Orlando Real! *¿Qué estás pensando?* I'm going to tell Abuelita. She'll never let you go out again." They could hear Pandi's loud voice behind them somewhere. She was the youngest, and she took her role of tattletale very seriously.

"Ay, *qué quehona* your sister is." His friends laughed but then began howling in pain. Pandi must have been hitting them with her heavy, scratchy backpack.

Anthony smiled at Olivia, and she felt the smile grow on her face, take over. Her siblings squabbled behind her, but she didn't even turn around to see what was happening, to tell them to quiet down. They became just a part of the bigger noise all around as she faced forward, with Anthony, watching the parade. The astronauts from *Apollo 12*, the main attraction, came by, waving. Olivia strained to see them, to take in every movement. These were men who had walked on the moon! Heroes. The crowd went crazy, and Olivia screamed along with everyone else, her own cry filling her ears, her head. Her palms stung from clapping. Anthony was cheering right along beside her, his arm pressed against hers.

The moon didn't seem so far away.

That evening, Anthony Rowe came to spend the night on their front lawn.

"Someone tell me again, why is a boy sleeping in our front yard?" Abuelita wiped the perspiration from her forehead and flipped the corn tortillas over the blue stove flame, her hand moving quickly. "Next thing you know, he'll be wanting to move in."

Olivia and Pandi exchanged glances. Anthony hadn't even asked to sleep inside in Orlando's room. He'd preferred to stay in the tent he hadn't had a chance to use at the parade, the boys being too lazy to set it up at the time.

"Orlando invited him," Pandi said, eyeing Olivia as they set the table for dinner. She puckered her lips and batted her long eyelashes, and Olivia widened her eyes at her. This was nothing to joke about in front of Abuelita.

"It doesn't matter who invited him," Abuelita said. "It's strange."

Abuelita was approaching eighty. Her hands were coarse from years of work, first at a ranch in Mexico, and then for many years in California, as a seamstress. She didn't work anymore; one of her sons had bought the house for her and the children. But she still woke up at four each morning for her rituals of cleaning, knitting, sewing, and cooking. She didn't have any friends and seemed to only tolerate having family over. "Doesn't the boy have his own home?" she asked. "He has to put that ugly thing on our front lawn?"

"He's a nomad," Orlando said, coming out of the hallway, reaching for the straw basket where she'd stacked the finished quesadillas.

Abuelita slapped his hand away. "Watch your language."

"No, we're learning about them in history. These ancient people who had no homes, just moved from place to place."

"What do they teach you in that school? Decent people live in homes. Not like bums in bags."

"They weren't bums, Abuelita."

"I'll tell him to go," Pandi offered.

Abuelita turned on her. "You want him to think we're not hospitable?" She looked Pandi up and down and then told Olivia, "Gorda, give the boy these," handing her the basket of quesadillas. Anthony had declined dinner at the table with the rest of them, but it seemed that Abuelita would still feed him.

Abuelita shook her head despairingly. "Nomads. Ay, *qué cosa.*"

Olivia approached the tent slowly, her shoes lightly treading the soft purple blossoms fallen from their jacaranda tree. She would have to rake them up, a job she enjoyed, along with gardening and anything to do with the outside.

Anthony put down his book when he saw her, and she presented the offering. "These are from my grandmother." She placed the basket on the ground, stood up, and took a step backward, as if he were some wilderness creature and needed space to explore the gift.

Anthony peered into the basket and waved back at the house grinning and whistling. Abuelita, who had been watching from inside, left in a huff. Olivia had never seen anyone dare to whistle at Abuelita before.

"Is that *the* Abuelita?" Anthony asked, with an amused smile. "Where's your mom?"

"She died when I was little."

He nodded and casually bit into one of the quesadillas. "You can have mine if you want."

This surprised her. "Where is your mother?"

"Back in Pennsylvania."

The screen door slammed, and Orlando came bounding toward them in the lumbering new walk he had adopted the past year. He was holding a paper bag. "She wants you," he told Olivia, and he walked right past her into the tent and sat down.

"Well, go on," Orlando said. "She's waiting." He had also picked up the custom of referring to Abuelita as "she."

"Gorda!" The voice of her grandma startled her.

"Goodnight," Olivia said.

"What does that mean, 'gorda'?" Anthony asked.

She wanted to leave, but his question kept her fixed to the ground.

"It's nothing. Just a name she has for me."

"A name?" He seemed genuinely interested, at least enough to stop eating.

She looked to Orlando for help, but he was engrossed in his paper bag.

"It's like if you were to call someone chubby." She ducked her head. "Or something like that."

She looked up, steeling herself, ready to see him reading his book or with his back to her, being friends with Orlando. But he hadn't moved. He was smiling. "If I was gonna call you something, it wouldn't be that."

There was a look in his eyes, a very particular one she'd seen in the eyes of boys at the bus stop. Almost like their parents hadn't fed them enough. She could ignore the silent hungry boys. She could even ignore the boys who whistled and said things like, "Hey, mamita," Pandi always speeding them both along. It's not like those guys expected a reply. But with Anthony . . .

"Olivia!"

She spun around and walked quickly back to the house.

In their bedroom that night, Pandi talked and talked. Olivia normally enjoyed her sister's stories. Pandi was so dramatic. A trip to the supermarket became an epic in her retelling. Olivia wanted to talk about the parade, but after ahhing over the astronauts for a few minutes, Pandi had no more to say about it and switched the topic to girls at school.

Olivia's mind wandered. She thought of the strange boy outside and his talk of college and books and a mother he was trying to get away from. He wasn't like any boy she had ever met. She thought of how perfect it would have been if they'd had a big beautiful rose garden. Then maybe Anthony would want to set up camp there all the time, and she could look out her window to see his pitched tent.

Anthony didn't need a rose garden. He kept coming to visit, although he left his tent back at his college dormitory. He started calling Olivia "Ollie Hardy," who was an old-time comedian, he told her. Olivia didn't mind so much until they watched one of his movies. She didn't see how being compared to a funny-looking fat man was supposed to be romantic. Still, he seemed to say it with some affection. When Anthony visited, Abuelita wouldn't speak to him, only watch the television in Spanish, telenovelas and these really old black-and-white movies that seemed cheesy but still made Olivia cry, every single time. If she teared up, Anthony would laugh at her, and so would Pandi. Pandi never cried about anything, only commented on how fake the women seemed and how they weren't that pretty if you really thought about it.

Anthony came bearing presents. Abuelita became suspicious of who he was visiting, her grandson or her granddaughter, and would complain about it when he wasn't around, only regarding him silently from her rocking chair when he tried to approach her while she made the transition from knit to purl. He didn't ask Olivia out on dates, didn't ask Abuelita for permission for anything. He just came whenever he wanted.

That spring, for her graduation, Anthony brought her a piñata. A pink and yellow donkey. He said they would "open" it later, and she hid it under her bed to avoid having to explain its presence to Abuelita. It made her nervous, keeping it down there. She had trouble sleeping that night.

It was not that she hadn't ever disobeyed Abuelita before. She'd become used to disobeying her in very small, precise ways that had already become ritual by the time she met Anthony Rowe. She and Pandi weren't allowed to shave, so she would take a knife from the kitchen into their bedroom and, with a bottle of lotion, shave her legs with the bare blade. She wasn't supposed to have an eyelash curler either, so she would use a tablespoon. But she knew the piñata was something different.

Orlando found the piñata looking for some change he'd dropped. He was spending a lot of time in her room these days. Before she'd known Anthony, she didn't have much contact with boys at all, including him. But now her brother was taking more of an interest in her. They would all go out together—it was the only way Abuelita allowed her to leave the house. Or, even when it was just the two of them at home, he would come into her room and sit on the floor.

"Where did this come from?" he asked.

"Anthony gave it to me."

"Anthony gave it to me," he mimicked. He always made fun of how she refused to call him "Tony," like everyone else.

"Doesn't he know you're a *viejita?*" he teased her. Laughing, he shook the donkey. "Hey, it's full!"

"Orlando—" Olivia warned.

"C'mon, Ollie. I'm hungry. There's only fucking tortillas and butter to eat."

"Ay, Orlando, *cállate.*" Abuelita wasn't around. She and Pandi were out shopping and wouldn't be back for hours. But Orlando still needed to break his habit of swearing. If Abuelita heard it, she'd take out her belt. Orlando always said it didn't hurt, getting whipped by an old lady. But it bothered Olivia.

"We should wait for Anthony," she said. "He's coming by today."

"So we'll save some for him."

Orlando bolted to the front yard and Olivia followed, standing by helplessly while he strung up the donkey. Someone pulled up, but it was just a bunch of Orlando's friends in their old gardening truck.

"Hey, guys! We got a burro," Orlando called to them. The boys cheered and poured out of the truck, their sneakers thudding on the concrete.

"Orlando," Olivia tried again.

His friends couldn't let him swing without wearing a blindfold, so one of the guys took out a bandana, and they tied it around Orlando's head and spun him around.

Anthony pulled up as Orlando was turned loose. "What's going on?" he asked, walking up the driveway.

"Is that Tony?" Orlando grinned, finally tapping the piñata. His friends hadn't brought him to it. "She don't mind if I take a swing at it. You can hit after. Ollie here can't down a piñata to save her life. Ever since we were kids." Before anyone could say anything else, Orlando knocked one of the donkey's hind legs off, and there was the sound of glass breaking.

Orlando pulled off the bandana and his jaw dropped to match the faces of his friends. A small heart-shaped bottle lay broken on the ground, a smell like roses heavy in the air.

One by one the boys looked at Anthony, fearfully almost, as if the explanation for the bottle of perfume were something sinister, ungodly. Orlando was the first to crack a smile, and then the boys erupted into hysterical laughter, clutching their stomachs, falling over. Olivia felt a flush come over her face.

"Get out of here!" she yelled.

Orlando was doubled over in laughter. She wrenched the bat out of his grip and waved it threateningly. "That's enough! ¡Váyanse!" The boys ran to the truck. Once they'd screeched around the corner, she realized she had been screaming at full volume. Trembling, she smoothed her hair back. Anthony was just looking at her like he never had before, like she was a different person. The donkey was still swinging a little, still wearing its silly smile.

"Piñatas are for candy, you know," she said. "For little kids' parties. You break them open with this." She held up the bat. It felt good in her hands, heavy and smooth. She tipped it to lean on her shoulder.

"But thank you," she added. "I would have liked it."

Anthony walked to the puddle and crouched, dabbing at the widening pool of perfume. When he stood up, he came close to her and drew his finger across her collarbone. She smiled, looking down at his shoes, thinking for one fleeting moment that he might be sliding a granule of glass across her skin. If he was, she would bear it. But nothing cut her. It was only Anthony's finger, warm and wet, moving over her.

"I know what a piñata is for," Anthony said in a low voice. "I thought, hey, you're a big girl now. Maybe you'd like something besides candy."

Olivia didn't know what to say to that. If he could take something so ordinary and make it new, what else was he capable of? And in turn, what did that mean she was capable of?

"You want to see what else is in this?" He moved behind her and placed his hands over hers on the bat.

She swallowed and was finally able to speak, with him behind her, not gazing at her with those blue eyes. "Anything else breakable?"

He laughed and to treasure it, she continued. "I won't get all cut up, will I?"

"No, nothing else. But it's a good thing your brother didn't knock out the lingerie. He would have beat the shit out of me."

"What!" Olivia could feel her face heating up, not sure whether she objected to the idea of lingerie or the curse word more.

"Well, they're wrapped up. Guess what color they are." He placed a kiss on her bare shoulder.

"I thought there was no such thing as color," Olivia said, trying to recover, to decide how she should react to this news, to his lips on her skin.

"Hm?" Anthony said, moving his arm around her waist. "Who said that?"

"You did. You said that the day I met you."

Anthony lifted his head. "Well, for you, there is. Any color you want."

"Really?"

He burrowed his face in her neck, and she felt the pressure of his lips there. "Really," he said, coming up and kissing her hair, smoothing some stray strands behind her ear.

She slowly relaxed back into him, the piñata dangling before her, full of what other surprises she wondered. Sister Bernadette had said piñatas were symbols. You were to attack them as you would your own sins. Anthony squeezed her tighter, gently pulling the bat from her hands.

When Abuelita and Pandi got back from the market, she and Anthony were sitting in the front yard, playing cards. The piñata, whole except for one leg, was hidden back under her bed.

The Desert in Green

The first time I met Miguel, he was climbing a fence. He had a backpack—brown, with a big green patch sewn over one side of it. It wasn't the dark green of our uniforms. More like grass. I remember thinking, as I told him to get down, that it was the first time in days, maybe weeks, that I had seen that color.

"You caught me," he said in Spanish, hopping down and upsetting the dirt. He held up his hands, not over his head, but forward, his palms open to the sky.

I checked him out and reported the pickup on the radio. "*¿Quieres agua?*" I asked, handing him a bottle out of the supply I kept on the passenger side. They could always use water.

"*¡El Negro habla español!*" he said, pleased. Most people are surprised to hear the first few words come out, my accent natural, the rhythm smooth. Spanish was my first language, spoken to me by my Tijuana-born mother at home. But they don't know that. It takes them a second to catch on, to understand that language coming from this black skin. I can actually see their growing ease as they take in my expressions, even my body language. I'm familiar to them.

I had only been on the job a few months when I met Miguel. I'd run

23

down a few guys, ducked a few punches. I'd never fired my gun, except in practice.

Since high school, I'd held several security jobs. At hotels, museums, and the like. Those usually involved asking elderly men to step back from paintings and locating misplaced digital cameras. I even had my stint as a bouncer at a strip joint, making good enough friends with the girls so that I developed a dislike for going as a customer, earning boos from the guys who went to the ones in nearby Mexicali.

But Border Patrol, this homeland security, was something different. Following the rules. Keeping the law. These were things that had always seemed so straightforward. When I was a kid, my mom would have to pull me away from reading the rules posted at public swimming pools and parks. She said I was born to be a cop.

The second time I caught Miguel was like running into an acquaintance on the street. "*El Negro todavía habla español*," he said, and I laughed. A lot of people, on both sides of the border, called me El Negro. I recognized him by his smile and that same brown and green-patched backpack. Also, my brother's name was Miguel.

I waited with him while they did the routine background check at the station. He unzipped his backpack and withdrew a sketchbook. He closed the backpack very quickly, even though we'd already searched it, all his belongings spread out on a table. "*Es el desierto. Esto también.*"

The pages showed landscapes of the desert. By just handling them, he was getting powder on his fingers. Yellows, purples, greens, and reds. But they were the kinds of drawings where it didn't matter if things got smudged. I listened to Miguel talk about them. I spent a lot of my time watching the desert of the Imperial Valley. Of course, my job was to find things in it. I was trained to respond to movement, whistles in the dark. Miguel's drawings made me think of being in the desert without the watching and the waiting part. Or, a waiting of a different kind.

A lot of the guys crossing make connections along the way. The groups I found could have from three to thirty guys. They devised simple strategies, involving lookouts and diversions. But Miguel was always alone. He said you couldn't trust those other men. You had to rely on yourself. And doing that, you were able to hear God speak to you. "Even in the desert," is what he said.

It wasn't anything unusual, me running into Miguel again. I'd heard of other guys finding repeat offenders. It happened all the time. Sometimes twice in the same day. And a lot of the guys weren't that surprised or upset when you caught them. They knew what they were up against. And they knew it was your job to bring them in. That was my view of it, anyway.

Like I joked with Miguel, when he stopped talking about his drawings, worry settling into his eyes, "*No te preocupes*. You're just getting practice."

It was after the third time I'd seen Miguel when another agent, Jones, asked me, "Why do you talk that way to them, Clark?"

We were in the locker room. All other conversations stopped.

"Talk what way, Jones?"

Jones was a tall white boy from St. Louis. We'd only talked at length once, during orientation. "You know. Like you're encouraging them."

I'd been looking through my gym bag for my socks. I set the bag on the floor of the locker. "How do I do that?" I asked, and turned to face him.

His nose was sunburned, something the guys would tease him about. He laughed a little, still facing his locker, and shook his head. "Forget it."

"No, tell me." I said. "Is it the jokes, the Spanish? Maybe it's the water. Maybe we shouldn't give them any, and then they wouldn't be encouraged."

He stopped doing whatever it was he'd been pretending to do—I could tell I'd made him angry by the way his whole body stiffened.

"I didn't mean it like that, all right? Don't put your issues on me."

"My issues?" I almost wanted to laugh. Some of the other guys did. I think I'd said "issues" in my white man accent. I was the jokester, the guy they got to go charm girls at clubs.

But then Jones said, "You know what I mean. About your mom." He said it with such damn solemnity.

Like a flash, my good humor was gone, and I wanted nothing more than to punch him in his stupid, solemn face.

"Clark." It was Quincy, our supervisor, calling. His office was located off the short hall leading to the locker room, close enough that he could hear every word if he lowered the talk radio. "Can I see you in my office?"

Jones was facing his locker again, still red-faced, but no more so than before. I shut my locker with a firm push and followed Quincy to his office.

"Have a seat," he said and closed the door.

I still had my towel around my neck. I pulled it onto my lap. I had always prided myself on keeping my temper, but I noticed the sting in my palms as my hands gripped the damp towel.

Quincy was a stout man in his fifties. He preferred tequila to beer. "Different agents have different perspectives," he said. "Let Jones have his opinions. You're both doing the same work."

I must have looked doubtful because then he asked, carefully, "Are you sure you want to be here, Clark?"

"Sir?"

"You're one of our best agents. No one's questioning that. The Patrol can depend on you. But I'll ask you again. Are you sure you want to be here?"

"You wouldn't be asking Jones that or any of those other guys in there."

"You're not any of those other guys, are you, Clark?"

I looked up, searching his face for accusation, or worse, pity. But all I saw was the sincerity I'd come to expect from him.

"No, sir." And it felt like the first time I'd admitted it to anyone, even my family, even myself. "But I do want to be here," I assured him.

Quincy nodded. "It's a tough job. . . ."

"But somebody's gotta do it."

He smiled and held out his hand. "Very good, Agent Clark. Enjoy your day."

Months passed, and it was the usual pickup and chase routine. I didn't see Miguel. Sometimes I wondered if he had made it across. Or maybe he was saving money for another trip.

But I didn't have to wonder anymore when Sterling came up to me in the cafeteria one day. Tina Sterling was on BORSTAR, the rescue squad, and one of the few women in the Patrol. She was wearing her short brown-blond hair up, like she did when she whipped our asses at pool.

"Hey, it's the thief Sterling," I said, referring to her stealing a base at our softball game last weekend. The guys had been harping on her all week. Made us feel better because it seemed that Tina was good even at games she'd never played before.

"Hey, Noél." She swung one leg over the bench in her usual easy manner and sat down. But she didn't quip back. "Javier was on detail last week," she said, rubbing at something on the table. "They came across this guy out there. Collapsed, you know the story."

I did. A lot of the border-runners were moving east, trying to cross over where there was less of a Patrol presence. The trouble was, it was the desert that caught them then. The desert may have been free of laws and judgments, but it didn't shelter, and it didn't care.

"Yeah?" I took another bite of my sandwich, although I could feel my appetite slipping. I wanted to pretend it was someone else. It could have been anyone else. I could have gone on thinking he'd made it somehow, finally got to wherever he'd wanted to be.

But Sterling never let a guy off easy. She took a folded piece of paper out of her pocket. "I took this from his bag after he died at the station. You know how they get rid of their things if there's no contact address." I could see the smears of chalk on the paper. A swirl of fingerprints in bright blue. I wasn't ready to take it, and she didn't push. I was so grateful that I couldn't think of what to do except throw a smile so she wouldn't worry too much. "The thief Sterling."

The fact was I told people no all the time. I took out my gun. I knocked guys to the ground. I put their hands in cuffs. I said no in so many ways.

I'd picked Miguel up, turned him in. Three times. But had I really told him no? Maybe he would have been better off if I had. If I'd told him, in English or Spanish, to pack up his fucking drawings and go home. We didn't want him. But there was something in Miguel I couldn't say no to. I couldn't go into his heart and stamp out the desire, the hope that there was even the slightest possibility of him helping his family. My badge didn't extend that far, and even if it did, would I want that job?

My mother was a college graduate. Been working since she was fourteen years old. She applied for her citizenship as an adult and now voted in every election. But once she was just a little girl holding the papers of her cousin as if they were hers, grinning like a Cheshire cat as she recited the lines her parents had trained her to repeat to the nice American officers. She'd made it across, married one now-deceased black man, and given birth to three Americans: my sister Irma, my brother Miguel, and me. And I'd be lying if I said I wasn't grateful.

I went home the week after I found out about Miguel. Drove straight to Legg Lake Park, where the family was having an *asado* to celebrate my *tío* Felix's fiftieth birthday. When I pulled up in the parking lot, it was dusk and a bunch of my uncles were standing around a grill, drinking Tecate.

I checked under my seat to make sure my gun was secure. They recommend we carry it on us all the time, in case we run into a familiar face. I'd thought it was a joke when they'd told us that at orientation, but they weren't kidding. They said you'd be surprised who you could run into at your local *taquería*, at the liquor store down the street. But I didn't like carrying it with all the kids around. I'd become comfortable with it, but it still felt heavy. It never stopped feeling heavy.

"Noél! Noél's here!" My uncles called from behind the spice-filled cloud, the smell of *carne asada* on the air.

They used to joke about me being *la migra*. But once Tío Pedro came to me, asking for help for a friend. When I refused, not even wanting to hear the details, he just looked me in the eyes and said, "Okay. No problem, *hombre*." And he patted my shoulder, no hard feelings. My uncles didn't laugh about me being la migra after that. I guess they found out it wasn't the joke they had thought it was. I didn't even really meet them until I was in junior high, after my dad died. Then it was okay for them to come over. It was okay for Mom to let them in, okay for them to help us out. When my dad died, ten new dads took his place.

I got out of the car and hugged and shook hands with them all. My mother was setting up the tables, yelling after the kids.

I went and kissed my mom. "Where's Angelina?"

"*Allá*, on the swings." She pointed to a little playground. "Dinner's almost ready. Tell her to come eat."

"All right. Hey, Angie girl!"

"Uncle Noél!" Miguel's little girl pumped her skinny legs harder and jumped off the swing, landing firmly in the sand. "Where were you?"

"At work, Miss Nosy." I scooped her up and sat on the low brick wall surrounding the sand.

"Did you bring me a present?"

Sometimes I'd bring her little souvenirs from Mexico. She liked the dolls and wooden toys. She'd never been there.

"No, but I've got something better."

"Oh."

I laughed at her disappointed tone and took Miguel's drawing out of my pocket.

"What is that?" Angelina asked.

"*Es el desierto.* Don't you know the desert when you see it?" I teased her.

She yawned and laid her head on my chest. "The desert isn't green," she pouted.

"*A veces sí, mija,*" I said, hugging her close. "Sometimes, for some people, it is."

Forces

Her regular doctor had said you got them by wearing shoes that were too tight, shoes that crunched the toes into a point. But the podiatrist had said some people were already more inclined to get them than others, that it was hereditary. Nothing you could do about it, not really.

"I don't see anything."

"Right there!" Andi pointed to her foot, already extended for Gabe to see, to where the bone jutted out below her big toe. She'd first noticed the bump about a few months ago, just looking down at her feet one day, one beside the other.

"Is that it?" Gabe asked. He set the tray on the pool table and put his hands in his pockets. His forehead crinkled into a frown.

"What do you mean, 'is that it'? It's huge! Here, it's easier to see if you compare." She drew her foot back.

He scratched his head. "Gross."

"Shut up."

"Bunions." Gabe straightened and began transferring the balls to the triangle, holding two to three between his fingers as he arranged them into alternating stripes and solids. He moved the front point of the triangle to the worn spot in the felt and carefully lifted it off the table with a grace he reserved for this game and bowling.

"Aren't those what old ladies get, bunions?" he asked.

"That's what I was thinking when the doctor told me. Isn't that what old ladies get. I wanted to cry."

"You're gay."

"It's never gonna be the same, you know. It makes me think about mortality."

"What does a pimple make you think about? Plague?"

"I'm not kidding. This is it for me, the beginning of the end."

Gabe just turned around and walked away from her to choose a cue. He had always walked with a limp, ever since she first met him in high school. So no matter how tough he acted or even when he said stupid things to rile her up, her anger always softened when walking beside him.

"I'm deformed," she said, trailing him. "I saw photos on the computer. I can show them to you."

"No! Let's play, Quasimodo. That is if you don't have any bells to ring tonight."

Gabe was the only one of her South El Monte friends she'd told about the newfound bunion, probably the only one she would tell. He was just one of those friends you told embarrassing things to, for the comical horror in his face, but mostly for the way it would dissipate into a smile. In a matter of seconds you would see whatever you were worried about acknowledged, and then, poof, gone, just like that.

They'd been at the parish fiesta, standing by the bumper cars, out of ride and food tickets, when Gabe suggested going to their old hangout, the pool hall behind the Jack in the Box on Durfee.

It was a lot more crowded than it was during the week. During the week, it was mostly older men, Andi usually being the only female in the establishment.

"I'm calling, but you can have sappos if you want," Gabe said.

"Ah, sappos." She leaned back against the table and folded her arms over her chest. "I think that half my shots must be pure luck."

Andi preferred not having to call her shots. She figured calling was just doing what you were going to do anyway, but telling everyone else first what you wanted to happen. It made more sense to her when your intentions weren't obvious. Like when you needed to use one ball to knock another ball in. Or when you needed to get to your ball by bouncing off a wall. Still, she wanted credit for every shot she made, intentional and accidental.

Gabe, on the other hand, just loved showing off.

He was already lining up to break. He always did a better job than she did, so she left him to it, grabbing a cue and settling on a stool. Gabe had rolled his cue on the table, but she figured she'd take her chances.

"The professionals call every shot," Gabe said. The balls broke with a satisfying crack. He didn't sink any. It was still open.

"Are we professionals?" she asked.

"The Olympic team from South El Monte." Gabe cupped his mouth. "*¡La gente se vuelva loca!*" He let out a *grito*.

Some men from the neighboring table called out, "*¡Ándale!*"

Andi put her face in her hands.

"Let's see who's the king of pool tonight," Gabe said.

"Or queen," she reminded him, popping out from her hands.

He rolled his eyes. "And you know, if you're trying to disable me with cheesiness, it won't work. I've built up a resistance."

He yelled that Mexican yell again.

"*Híjole*," she said, borrowing the phrase from her mother.

Then to show him she meant business, she cleared her throat. She took perspective from the white ball and looked out at her options, decided that the two ball looked most appealing, and aimed for the far right pocket. It rolled in. "Solids," she sang.

Gabe's eyes widened, and he gave her an approving nod. "Look who's back."

She smiled at him and chose her next shot. She would have had to lead with her other hand, so she moved the cue behind her back to shoot. "This game sure calls for strange positions."

"But I thought those were your favorite kind."

When she gave an exaggerated gasp, Gabe said, "Come on, that was way too easy."

"I see how it is."

Andi steadied the cue and made the shot. She circled the table, eyeing the white ball, then looking to the others.

"Am I gonna get to play this year?"

She took more time in selecting her shots than he did. "Hold your horses."

She missed the next shot. "Rats. I haven't played in forever," she said, pulling the cue from its horizontal position to stand tall beside her.

"Don't they have pool halls in New York?"

"I went to a place once." She frowned. "But it wasn't like this. The people were dressed up like they were going out. And there were all these young people. Mingling."

"You don't say."

"Yeah. A pool night is a cheap night. It's not about being stylish or meeting new people."

"Admit it, if there aren't a lot of middle-aged to elderly drunk Mexican men around, you just can't enjoy yourself, can you, Andi?"

"Call me crazy."

Gabe just smiled and studied his next shot.

They'd been coming here for years. Since she started college in New York, she liked coming back during her vacations. It felt like old times here, like nothing ever changed. And it didn't need to. All you needed was to be able to play.

The walls were mostly bare except for a few tequila and beer advertisements with women in bikinis and surf in the background. The light fixtures were suspended by chains over each of the tables. The carpet was hard like concrete. The music alternated between classic rock and *ranchera*. Robert Plant's wail and accordion music equally suited the place.

Gabe crouched to see the balls at eye level. He leaned back, one hand holding on to the table. Then he rose and aligned his body with the cue. Gabe's shots were fast, cracking bolts. The balls didn't roll, but slid, slick over the faded green felt. When he missed a shot, it was usually because he was hitting too hard.

"You'll be back for Christmas, right? You could help design the set for the church play. They need people. To paint and whatever. It's gonna be good. Remember when I acted in that Easter play?"

"I remember how your goat kept chewing on your robe," Andi said. "Where did they get those animals anyway? Someone must rent them out, for theatrical purposes."

"That goat made me mad. It wouldn't walk where I wanted it to. I had to yank on it the whole time, so I had no idea what was going on. And it stepped on my foot. Like hard!"

"He really got your goat, huh?"

Gabe narrowed his eyes. "Resistance."

The Easter in question, Gabe had performed in a Spanish Passion play. It was held in Industry Hills at an equestrian center. The set was built on the rodeo arena and gave the facades of various key places: the Roman palace, the Last Supper room, the Jewish Temple. The crowd, seated on the bleachers, got to scream, "¡Crucifícalo, crucifícalo!" And if things got too dull, or if they gave up on trying to understand what Jesus and Pontius Pilate said as they passed the microphone back and forth, they could go buy holographic pictures of the saints in gold frames, rosaries. Could go eat sticks of roasted corn on the cob slathered in mayonnaise and chile.

"Do you still keep in touch with Satan?" Andi asked.

Gabe frowned and scratched his chin. "I thought you did."

"Hey!" She waved her cue at him like a spear.

"Nah." He cracked a smile. "I don't know what happened to that fool. He got into movie extra work or something. Never heard from him again."

"Maybe he got discovered."

"More like undiscovered."

"He was so dramatic. I wasn't sure if he was supposed to be Dracula or something. He kept laughing all villainously." She imitated the maniacal laugh. "Why was Satan in the play anyway? Is he usually?"

"Someone on the planning committee must have seen *The Passion* too many times. Speaking of the devil."

Gabe had set down his cue and was looking beyond Andi's shoulder. She saw his arm first. Pete Villegas, with a girl behind him.

"Hey, man," Gabe said.

"Hey, guys. This is Janine. From choir." Pete looked at Andi. "I didn't know you were back in town."

"She's been here two weeks," Gabe said.

"Right," Pete said, though it didn't sound like he thought there was anything right about it.

"Andi, Janine." Pete made a weak gesture of introduction.

"Nice to meet you," the girl said with a smile that showed all her teeth. She clutched a big white teddy bear.

"Nice to meet you." Andi was still holding her cue, so she shook with her left hand.

"Andi," Janine tried out the name and must have found it lacking. "Is your name short for anything?"

People often asked her this, and she had yet to come up with a better answer than the disappointing, "No," or the plucky but usually confusing, "My dad didn't believe in derivation," which was true, incidentally. She shook her head. "Nope, that's it."

"It's so cute."

"Let us finish up this game, yeah? Then we can play teams," Gabe said.

Pete nodded, and they set their stuff down. Andi tried not to look at them as they murmured to each other.

She missed her next shot, and Gabe made the rest of his in, getting the eight ball in on the first try, a corner shot. They knocked cues. "Good game," Gabe said, and Andi leaned her cue against the wall.

"Team time," Gabe said.

They didn't verbally assign teams, but Janine moved closer to Pete and that was that.

"So what have you guys been doing tonight?" Pete asked, chalking up his cue. He was wearing a faded black shirt with an indecipherable screen-print image that had cracked and peeled in a million places. He didn't look dressed for a date. But then Andi had never seen him on an ordinary date, just with steady girlfriends. There was no gel in his hair, and it had an unkempt quality that she remembered from times in bed. Gabe didn't know she could have made the association. At least, he didn't let on he did. Maybe Janine knew, female intuition rearing its head. Or maybe Pete had told her.

Andi waited for Gabe to answer, but Pete was looking at her. "I don't know, nothing much," she said. She slowly rotated the chalk on the end of her cue and rubbed at the blue it left on her hands.

"Uh oh. Andi's already having blackouts," Gabe teased. He made a

36

drinking sign to Janine and winked. He had this way of including people. That's one of the things she had first noticed and liked about him.

"She's Irish, you know," Gabe added.

"Don't say that." Andi usually liked it when her Irish heritage was pointed out. But she didn't like how the conversation had come to focus on her, in front of this Janine girl.

"Why not?" Gabe asked. "You are, aren't you?"

"Yeah. But every time you tell people I'm Irish, I end up with my head in a toilet somewhere."

"What is that, an Irish fairytale?"

Andi shook her head. "Terrible."

Janine stood by the table, smiling. Something in her posture suggested waiting. Waiting for what, Andi couldn't tell, but she sensed it had something to do with her. The men playing cards laid out their hands and erupted in a burst of clapping and laughing.

"That reminds me," Andi said. "Want a drink?" She grabbed her small wallet from where she'd set it on a stool, and stuck it into the back pocket of her jeans, her keys dangling from the attached key chain.

"Here, I'll give you money," Gabe offered.

"Nah, I owe you."

"Cool. Get a pitcher, yeah?"

"You got it." She didn't wait to hear from anyone else, just walked to the front room.

It was packed. A group of younger people had come, including some girls. Andi placed her forearms on the bar. A sign read, IN GOD WE TRUST. EVERYONE ELSE PAY CASH.

"Hey, sweetheart. You're not smiling." It was the owner.

"Oops." She put one on.

"That's the stuff. What would you like, sweetheart?"

"A pitcher of Bud, please." Bud and Bud Lite were all they had here. She and Gabe liked stronger, better beer, but they didn't complain. The pitchers made up for it.

A little television set perched above the bar gave a black-and-white view of the parking lot outside. The barstool in front of her was torn, and she placed one finger into the yellow foam, withdrawing it quickly because it felt too intrusive and a strangely gross action, to be feeling the foam of this torn stool.

"How many glasses, honey?"

"Two?"

He set before her a glass pitcher and two frosted mugs he'd pulled out of the little fridge behind him. He was pushing forward the glasses when he stopped and squinted at her. "You twenty-one?"

"Yeah, don't you remember?"

"Let me see some ID." He smiled, as if asking more out of curiosity. She fished her license out of her beat-up wallet and handed it to him. He held it up close to his eyes. Two men sitting at the bar laughed. "*¿Te da pena contar?* Do you need to take off your shoes? And pants?"

They laughed at the joke as it came to them, like a joke will when it has a good place like a bar to roll along.

"Here you go, sweetie." The owner handed back her ID and shot the men a look.

Andi looked back toward the table through the big doorway. Pete was standing with his hands in his pockets. He caught her eyes and walked over to her. He made to take the pitcher, but she said, "I got it."

Her right foot ached a little when she stepped on it. This ground was hard, the carpet worn through.

"So you're back," he said.

"Yeah."

"You could have called me."

"Well, we're hanging out now, right?" She walked quickly back to the pool table. The huge teddy bear occupied almost the entire nearby table. She set the pitcher by its furry crotch, giving an obligatory glance Janine's way.

But Janine didn't notice. She was talking to Gabe. "There are a lot of guys here," she said.

"It's a man's game," Gabe spoke deeply. "We just let Andi tag along, let her think she's good. Oh, shhh, she's back."

Gabe joined her at the table.

"Can I serve you, ole buddy, ole pal?" she asked.

"Yes, woman, serve me up."

Smiling, she poured the pitcher into the tipped mug.

She knew Gabe. He'd never open a door for her; he'd always walk in first. He'd grab shotgun before she had a chance of calling it. He never excused himself when he sneezed or burped very intentionally. It was a matter of principle with him. But he was also one of the sweetest guys she'd ever met.

"She's cute, huh?" He motioned to Janine. "I hope he doesn't screw this up."

Gabe had never talked to her about Pete and girls before, and she struggled to keep her face passive. "Looks like he's doing fine," Andi said flatly.

"Go talk to her, see if she's interested."

"What is this, fourth grade?"

"You're such a snob, Andi. Go on." He nudged her in the side. "Make a friend."

"I came here to play pool, not make friends. Remember?"

"I remember," he admitted, but a little too quietly.

"You want a drink?" Pete asked Janine.

"Sure! Something with vodka?"

Pete and Gabe exchanged a smile. "I think they only have beer."

"Oh, I'll get something later maybe. I've never really liked beer. The taste gets to me. Oh, I'm so bad at this," Janine said as she hit the white ball directly into the far-side pocket. "I'm sorry." She covered her face.

It was Andi's turn. She had a choice between two shots. One was by a side pocket, the other was a longer shot. She preferred the farther one. The side ones seemed to require more finesse than she could usually muster.

Pete walked over to the other ball. "You could knock this in easy."

"Nah, I'm gonna go for that one."

"This'll set you up better. Just hit it high, right here." He pointed to the spot at the ball she should aim for, her cue still pointed toward the far ball in the corner.

"It's all right—"

"You just tap it light and—"

"You know, I have a partner," she said.

The light smile that had been playing on Pete's lips disappeared, and he backed away from the table. "Just trying to help."

She shot the white ball toward the end of the table but ended up completely missing—something she hadn't done yet tonight—the ball bouncing off the wall and rolling right back toward her. Everyone was quiet for a beat, Pete not even moving to take his turn. "I'll be right back," she said. She drank some beer before setting her glass on the table and leaving.

Hiding out in the restroom would only work for a little while. She used the toilet. She washed her hands with the pink liquid soap. They were out of paper towels, so she wiped her hands on the thighs of her jeans, feeling the cold come through. She avoided looking in the mirror. She didn't want to see her face.

She didn't want to go back to the table either. She wanted to sit at the bar, with the owner calling her sweetheart, and watch the silent black-and-white parking lot movie unfold. She wanted to see herself like that, from the outside. Pulling up her jeans, never meeting her own eyes. Perspectives usually unknown to her—the back of her head, her profile. No thoughts, no questions, because that's where the camera stopped. All it saw was movement and stillness.

It had been a summer ago. A summer ago Pete had been on top of her. She remembered the weight of him, her nose in his neck. He'd pulled down her panties, his eyes on her as he did it, his fingers moving down her thigh. He'd taken them off even though he'd felt before there was a pad stuck to them. She liked that, how he wasn't afraid of touching her, of being close to her. The pad had been white, just a precaution. She hadn't bled all day. So when he came up from her body with red on his white undershirt she'd been confused for a second, then had started laughing out of embarrassment. He went to the bathroom to wash it off, and she sat up, with her fingers in her mouth, listening to the faucet. She put her underwear back on, pushing the pad into herself, blotting, hoping he wasn't disgusted or upset. He'd been a good sport, as he was about most things. He came back to the room still wearing the shirt, the bottom part wet, all the blood washed out. She had said she was glad it was clean, and it wasn't until he had left and she lay in bed that night that she realized she'd lied.

The truth was she'd liked seeing him like that.

Andi unlocked the bathroom door and started back toward the table. She had to stop to let a man take a shot. Her foot was bothering her tonight. She felt a small ache when she stepped on it. She had shoe inserts from the podiatrist, but she couldn't wear them with flip-flops. They were supposed to help her walk better. It was weird to think she was stepping wrong, that she was messing up on something so simple.

Someone tapped her on the shoulder. "Your keys are falling out."

She could tell there was a man standing behind her. "Oh, they're fine," she said over her shoulder. He was talking about the keys on her wallet.

"You're very beautiful." The man had a heavy accent.

Andi smiled and nodded her head slightly. He was still standing there, not moving.

"Let me explain. I just want to say I'm in love with someone else. But I think you're very beautiful."

She turned around then. He was her height, and she caught his eyes right off.

But he had said what he wanted to say. He gave a little smile and then went back to his table.

The man in front made his shot and moved out of the way.

With her path clear, there was nothing for her to do but walk back toward the table, a small throb in every step. Toward Pete, his eyes worriedly on her as he twisted the chalk over his cue. Toward Gabe, pointing to a corner pocket. Toward Janine, her eyes trained on Pete, a calmness on her face.

"It's your turn," Gabe told her. "Still open."

Andi took up her cue, aiming for a cluster of stripes and solids. She hoped to sink something. She'd never been good at calling it.

The Bolero of Andi Rowe

The mariachis arrived just in time.

Their *trajes* were black with silver chains on the shoulders and running down the pant legs. They wore red bow ties, and their black velvet sombreros had red and silver threads making designs, fanning out over the dark velvet, a braid zigzagging along the rim and around the peak to end in tassels. The one with the violin case had a moustache. The other man was clean-shaven, with a build similar to that of the *guitarrón* case he was shuffling.

It was a Friday night in Uptown Whittier, the sun still dropping to the horizon. Beth had kicked him in the shin again, and unlike before, Pete Villegas stumbled, loosening his grip on her shoulders so that she for sure would have run out onto Greenleaf had it not been for the violinist's help in restraining her.

"Motherfuckers!" Beth's fair complexion had taken on an angry redness from all the screaming.

"*Señorita, cálmate,*" the man said, and the patience in his voice surprised Pete. It was like hearing a piano's tinkling in a *ranchera* song. Out of context.

"Let go of me!"

The violinist handed his small case to the guitarrón player, the shorter of the two men, so as to get a hold of Beth with both hands.

"You need help, sir?" he asked Pete.

"Thanks. I just want to get her home," Pete said, grateful.

In the entire time he'd been struggling with Beth, no one had offered help, to either of them. People had always said Pete had a kind face. Which perhaps explained why since the quarrel had started no one had mistakenly come to Beth's aid. For his part, he felt extremely conspicuous holding down a screaming, cursing blond girl in public. When they were dating, he had sometimes felt that they were being watched more closely somehow. It had never really bothered him before.

"She has drunk too much, huh?" It might have been a rude question, but the violinist said it kindly, like he understood.

"You could say that again."

Pete knew Beth was drunk the moment he laid eyes on her, walking alone on the curb. She was wearing the Dodgers shirt he'd bought her last summer and white shorts, her hair in a messy ponytail. It wasn't even dark yet, but she had that careless sway to her hips, that glazy look in her eyes. He hadn't seen her this bad in a long time. She didn't seem all that surprised to see him either. Just a little while ago he might have been meeting her here. He'd have looked for one of the slanted parking spots on Greenleaf, walked by the shops, maybe lingered at the windows of the cigar or record store, and gone into the bar to find her sitting on a stool, wrapping her long hair around her fingers, waiting for him.

But things were different now. When Beth recognized him, she started yelling, about how she'd been thrown out of a bar for hitting the artwork, how she hadn't done anything wrong. He'd tried to determine whether her friends were with her. Probably those worthless assholes she was renting the house on Walnut with. But he didn't see anyone, and he couldn't get a straight answer out of her. He didn't want to go inside to check and run the risk of her taking off on him.

At first, he'd merely tugged slightly on her arm, trying to coax her to his car. But as soon as she figured out he was trying to take her home, she'd said that she wasn't going anywhere with him, and the situation had quickly escalated. He was stronger than her, but she was nearly as tall, and it was clear she didn't give a damn about hurting him, or herself. She was too drunk to even yelp when she banged into a fire hydrant in a dart to escape his hold. And now she was using all the strength she had to fight him.

His car wasn't too far off, but there was no way he would have been able to drive with her in it. He didn't want to call a friend, and have him see her like this. It looked like his best option was to drag her, kicking and screaming, the distance to her house. A fast trip in the car, but who knew how long it would take walking with a less than willing companion. Pete had been mustering the energy to embark on the journey, when the two mariachis, like angels, emerged from around the corner. Amidst the tattooed rockabillies in their polka dots and flannel, they stood out. Pete knew right away they were the real deal. Professionals, with worn but clean cases, sharp, pressed suits, and the simple earnestness he'd associated with mariachis since childhood. Not like the group he'd played with in college. Kids who'd taken trumpet and violin lessons and were having some fun while going for their pre-med degrees. Hey, that's what Pete had been doing. When they had played, it'd been like no other feeling he'd known. Not his vocation maybe, but more than a hobby. Much more. He'd soon be in med school with all those other guys one of these days.

"Do you have a car?" the violinist asked Pete, the two of them now securing Beth.

"Over there, the gray Ford." Pete gestured across the street to where he'd parked his car in a diagonal beside a sweet black Cadillac.

The man looked disappointed. The car must have seemed too small to contain the raging Beth, not to mention their instruments. "Our van is just around the corner. If you want, we could give you a ride."

Beth twisted between them, breathing heavily. "Let go of me. Pete!" Her voice was going hoarse, and she seemed to be getting tired. But every now and then she'd yank back violently.

Pete considered the man's invitation. They were fellow musicians, his kindred. "That would be great," he told them. "I'm Pete." He couldn't extend his hand so he nodded.

"*Mucho gusto.* I'm León, and this is Ignacio. We are part of—"

"Pieces of—"

"—Los Reyes del—"

45

"—shit. Fucking—"

"—Mar."

"Nice to meet you," Pete said.

"Shitheads!"

"You guys from Jalisco?" Pete asked in Spanish.

"Yes! How do you know?"

"I can hear the accent. I have family there."

"I hope you die!"

"Really? In what part?"

They continued talking as they walked down Greenleaf. Ignacio, the guitarrón player, followed with the instruments, offering encouragement.

"Cuidado, la señorita es fuerte. Agárrele, agárrele."

"Why can't you just leave me the fuck alone?" Beth seethed. She sounded as though she were near tears.

"We're just taking you home, Beth. It'll be all right," Pete said. It's what he'd been saying all night.

"Is this your girlfriend?" León asked.

"Ex."

"Ah. Here we are."

They were approaching a Volkswagen minibus. Pete had never seen anything like it. The van was painted in wide panels of hibiscus orange and cactus green. Identical holographic pictures of Our Lady of Guadalupe were stuck somehow to the side panel, one after the other. As they got nearer, Pete saw even the windows had curtains of Our Lady.

Beth started pulling her weight backward, her heels digging into the ground. Pete wondered if she'd got a good look at the van. Beth was Lutheran.

At the van, Ignacio put down the instruments, and León said apologetically. "It is my nephew's. He is an artist."

Pete smiled. "Yeah, I got one of those in my family, too."

They tried buckling Beth into the backseat, but she wouldn't have it. Finally, they got her seated on the floor in the back, with Pete sitting behind her, pinning down her arms. That seemed to be the best arrangement. León started the van, and she quieted down, even laying her head back on Pete's shoulder. She'd finally exhausted herself. Pete breathed in her hair. Her skin smelled like cucumber. He hadn't been this close to her in months.

"Where do you live?" León asked from the front seat.

"I'm from South El Monte, but I'm living in Montebello right now."

"Oh, we play in Montebello. At the Quiet Cannon."

"Oh yeah?" Pete had been to the club there once.

"What were you doing in Whittier?" Ignacio asked.

Now that Beth was passed out, they could talk in peace. Pete couldn't see the men from where he was sitting. It was nice to not have to look anywhere. He closed his eyes and leaned his head back, their low, manly voices descending on him.

"I was looking for a record," Pete said.

"*¿De quién?*"

"Agustín Lara."

"Ah, yes. He is very good."

"Don't you already have him?" León asked.

"Yeah," Pete admitted. "It was for a friend."

The last time Pete had seen Andi Rowe was at the drive-in. Beth had broken up with him that spring, and once Andi got home from college for the summer, they started a Friday night ritual. They'd pick up tacos and *horchata* from the King Taco on Garvey. Pete would pack a cooler with ginger beer in the trunk. The first movie they'd start out by sitting outside, spreading a blanket on one of the asphalt inclines. Their bodies leaning forward, eating, listening to the sound coming out of the car radio until it got too uncomfortable. Then they'd move inside the car. When the first movie ended, they'd usually drive to another lot, where the least awful movie was showing. Then they'd go to the snack stand and buy popcorn, bringing it back to the car to have with the ginger beer. They'd eat the buttery, salty popcorn out of the bag between them. When their hands slowed, the bag would eventually be set aside. And then Pete would have his arm around her, and they'd be sitting close, thigh to thigh, his fingers kneading her far shoulder in slow, circular presses, until he could feel her melting under him, and then he'd start kissing behind her ear, coaxing little sounds from deep in her throat. He'd make his way to her mouth, soft and open to him, the faint spice of ginger on her tongue, and it would feel, at that moment, like the entire night and day and even Beth and every other girl before her were all just a prelude to this moment, where he was at long last kissing Andi Rowe. And there was nowhere else to go, except to keep going on as he was, deeper and deeper into her. And he would think, afterward, that's what happiness must have been. Like walking into quicksand and being sucked down whole, smooth and steady, knowing you were going somewhere, that struggle was useless, and that you would never be the same again.

This last time, before the kissing had started, Pete had turned off the radio on the movie and put on a CD of boleros instead.

"This is 'Solamente Una Vez,'" he told her.

"Didn't Elvis sing this song?" she asked.

"Yeah, the English version is 'You Belong to My Heart.' It was done first in Spanish."

Andi had her legs up, her bare feet on the dashboard. His plastic rosary dangled from the rearview mirror. He never removed it, even for the drive-in.

"They changed the title?" she asked.

"The words, too. You know that song 'Impossible' by Perry Como? That was actually 'Somos Novios.' What are you smiling about?"

"Nothing."

When the movie ended and they were kicked out of the parking lot, he drove her home, and they sat in the driveway, talking about a mysterious light they always noted beyond her garage. It was late, but in the unlikely event they called him to sub tomorrow, he'd just say he wasn't available. While they were talking, Andi's eyes, wandering, widened suddenly and she gave a small shriek.

"What is it?" Pete turned around, thinking she'd seen a burglar.

"A possum!" She pointed at the roof.

"Where?" He didn't see anything.

"It was right there!" She was shivering. "They're so gross! Worse than rats even."

"What's the big deal?" He poked her arm. It was funny seeing her so excited.

"They have scary eyes. And they lie with their bodies, pretending to be dead. I hate them!"

He'd had to calm her down before she could get out of the car, her squeaking turning into laughter and then finally subsiding, so she could breathe and he could take her mouth again.

By the time he had Beth all tucked into her bed, Pete felt sore all over, like he'd been hugging a hard metal bar with all his might.

"So what are you guys doing tonight?" Pete asked the men.

"Just going home. Ignacio's brother was getting married. Then he decided to cancel the wedding."

"I'm sorry."

"No, it's better this way. You see, his brother thought that by marrying this woman, he would get a chance at the money. But it turns out it was not the case. It was not about love. If it were, Ignacio would be there with his brother, drinking, singing the lonely songs. *Es verdad, ¿no?*"

Ignacio sighed good-naturedly. "What do you play?" he asked Pete.

Pete had told them he'd played in a mariachi band in college.

"Guitar for the band. And I play piano," he said.

"You know what's better than giving a girl a record," León said. "Giving her her own song."

Pete agreed, but he wondered how the man knew. He'd only said the record was for a friend.

He'd written a bunch of songs over the years. At least ten for Beth. He only wrote them after a fight, thinking that it would be the one to tip the scales, the one they could not come back from. When things were quiet, good, he felt no need to write. Sometimes, he would try to write something, for her birthday or Valentine's. But it was like the notes wouldn't come unless he felt broken inside.

After the mariachis dropped Pete off at his car, after they continued to talk about music and performing and their day jobs in a restaurant, it was around nine. It felt more like midnight. Tío was in the garage painting, the door open to the street. One of Pete's favorite things to do was to sit in that garage at dusk, when the whole lower world became a silhouette, kids running up and down the street playing, the sky above big and still blue.

Pete had been living at his *tío* Sebastián's house in Montebello for about six months. Tío's wife had left him five years earlier, and Tío still mourned the failed relationship as if she had died. Her picture was everywhere. Strangers had actually asked him, "When did your wife die?" It was the way he referred to her. Solemn, full of respect, and with finality. He'd been pretty bad off the first year. Drinking his Russian vodka alone. He went to buy it special. Didn't like going to bars because they never had the good kind, he said. Pete had offered to take him to a nice bar in West Hollywood. But Tío had said, "Oh no, I am too old for that." The other relatives couldn't take it. Mooning that much over a woman who'd gone off with another man. A fifty-year-old woman, acting like she was still young enough to do something like that. They thought he was the greatest fool.

It had been two years since Pete had graduated from college, and, at first, his mother had let him alone. But then she had started bugging Pete about when he was going to take the MCAT so he could finally go to med school like he'd promised. He defended himself by saying how was he supposed to study in a house full of people, with his nephews and nieces running around all hours. He shouldn't have brought the kids into it. The truth was he liked having them around. He liked coming home and having them rush him, always happy to see him. But he just needed some more time. He was content subbing at the El Monte district high schools. And singing with the church choir and working on his own songs. Going out in LA and Los Feliz and Hollywood, talking with whatever musicians crossed his path. He knew his mother didn't want him to leave really. She'd complained the whole time he was away at college, even though he came to visit almost every weekend. So he was surprised when she called his bluff and kicked him out, making him move into Tío's. Tío was the only relative living alone. An old bachelor. An artist. It was in this house of world music, incense, and countless works-in-progress that Pete was to study to be a doctor.

Tío kept the fridge in the garage well stocked with beer, in case anyone ever visited. Pete had never seen anyone come to visit in the whole time he'd been living there. This was why Pete never felt guilty about giving the beers to his friends. Tío would come down, say, "Oh, I need to restock," and he'd go through the motions of writing down on a pad all the needed beer, with such a concentration that Pete found it hard to look at him. Mexican and American beer. And now English, too, at Pete's request.

Tío came out from behind the easel and went to the fridge. "You look like you could use a drink," he said, smiling.

"That sounds right." Pete sat down on a wooden chair. "What's this you're working on?"

"It's my interpretation of another painting, by an anonymous Peruvian painter." He handed Pete the beer, grabbed his, and they clinked glasses. Tío settled down on a chair across from Pete. "There's this story that Satan painted a picture of Jesus suffering on the cross as a gift to his lover. He took a lot of time, getting in every detail."

Pete smiled at Tío's enthusiasm. He could get really worked up.

"He intended that they enjoy Jesus's suffering together. But when his lover saw the painting, she was so moved by what Jesus had gone through that she converted to Christianity."

"So it backfired?" Pete asked.

"Yes, Satan didn't get any that night."

"Is that a Harley jacket he's wearing?" Pete asked.

Tío shrugged. "He's the Prince of Darkness. He's gotta have good taste in clothes." They laughed. "You know what the moral is?"

Pete frowned. Tío didn't usually talk about morals, about neat little packages and things meaning this or that. "Be careful what you try to do nice for people?" he guessed.

"Could be," Tío said. "But I think it's more about how sometimes we just try too hard. Sometimes, *mijo*, it's just too much. Too much loss. Too much grief. Too much happiness."

Pete didn't really know what he meant. Maybe this was a new obsession, maybe Tío was going off on some kind of odd religious kick now. Aside from the painting of Christ, there were a few landscapes in the garage. Mostly there were paintings of skeletons. The skeletons were what people wanted, Tío had said. They're what sold.

So skeletons they got. Skeletons parading through streets, carrying spears with other skulls hanging heavy, jaws open, screaming smiles. Sailor skeletons and skeletons buying fruit and skeletons fighting with swords and hitting piñatas and eating barbecue and staggering along a *pueblo*, holding jugs and singing. Barber skeletons and mariachi skeletons, all of them going right on living, eating, drinking, holding onto their jobs, as if they were flesh and blood, as if everything was okay.

"My mom asks when you're going to stop painting these," Pete said, waving at them. He imitated her, speaking in Spanish, "If he did a nice one of *La Virgen* or something pretty like that, I'd buy it. I wouldn't even ask for a discount. *Pago el precio regular.* And put it in my salon."

"Ay, Gloria," Tío said, shaking his head. They both laughed at the imitation of his mother. The salon was her dream job. She was content to spend her days amongst styling products and mounds of slippery fashion magazines, making women look and feel prettier. Pete had once tried showing her one of his anatomy textbooks, and she'd made a face, saying only it was good that he would help people. But he felt a kinship with Tío. They both knew that the real matter of life, its guts, wasn't pretty. It was something more essential than that.

Tío's chuckles subsided, and he looked reflective. "I've never painted the Virgin, *niño*."

Pete was going to object, but he couldn't remember ever having seen a painting of Mary in the house. "No, Tío? Why not?"

Tío said it matter-of-factly, as if Pete were foolish not to know the reason. "I'm not worthy."

"Come on, Tío. You could paint her. It'd be beautiful." Pete took a swig of beer.

Tío smiled, but it wasn't his usual smile. It was too tight, like when the relatives asked him if he was still painting. They may as well have been asking him if he was still breathing. "When I am ready," he said.

And the way he said it, he made Pete feel like Tío had never made him feel—like a little boy.

The ranchera club was in Pico Rivera. He and Beth used to go there all the time, in the beginning. She hadn't danced or listened to ranchera music before he'd taken her there. He could remember the first time, how he'd held her hand and led her through the space. It had felt as though he had created it all for her, like a gift. Now he came alone, needing to hear the band, to be there.

The walls were still covered in black-lit paintings. They showed a landscape of a pink mountain range and green valleys. Men dressed like cowboys rode on horses and women dipped tin pails into a small river, their blouses hanging off their shoulders as if the next moment the thin fabric would slip, revealing their ample breasts.

Another wall had paintings of bottles of tequila dotted with purple asterisks, twinkling like stars.

Pete ordered a beer from a waitress, remembering after she left that he'd always sipped from Beth's margarita, too. The waitresses still wore what Beth had called their "ranch porno" outfits. White, low-cut, long-sleeved shirts and little black shorts with suspender straps. The waitresses, without exception, had big chests, small waists, and round bottoms. *Botellas de Coca-Cola*, as his friend Gabe would say. But he had loved Beth's body. A robust girl, he'd teased her. Small breasts and a bigger bottom. Strong legs. The body of an athlete.

When the song was over, the couples turned toward the stage and clapped. He always loved that part. The band was leaving, but the singer said they'd be back. The DJ came on then, and a dance song burst from the speakers on both sides of the stage. More couples flooded the dance floor. One couple stood out. The woman was tall and slender, with a wave to her body like that inherent in feathers or the spines of leaves. She wore a thin dress and a stoic expression. The man twirled and spun her in controlled, graceful movements. They looked as if they could have gone on dancing like that forever. Tireless like that. A less experienced couple bumped into them, the girl briefly entering their space. Their inertia unbroken, the man spun his woman to the other side of the room.

It was a large room, with a lot of long tables and chairs, like you'd find at a school cafeteria. A bull-riding program was showing on the TV screen. On the bottom of the screen were the words "Toros y Muerte."

The men became rag dolls on the bulls' backs, their bodies flailing in a stiff way, one arm raised high so they wouldn't touch the bull. Once a man was thrown, a group would come rushing into the arena. They would pull the man to safety and rope back the bull. Sometimes if the bull ran by the gate, the rider would just climb off its back, holding onto the rails. One guy got a little trampled, and when they'd run the bull off, he was still lying motionless.

"He's not even twitching," a man said at another table. And the men half-laughed, half-groaned out of pity.

They had to drag that guy out.

It was hard to watch something like this. If Pete concentrated on the men, his body tensed, anticipating their inevitable pain. Everyone knew they would fall. It was just a question of when. His eyes moved to the bulls, the way they spun in place, their backsides flying up as if pulled by a string. They were surprisingly flexible, powerful. His stomach unclenched. If he concentrated on the bull, it was okay.

Tomorrow Beth would go to his tío's house. She'd walk right into Pete's room and say "Oh my God," rapidly unbuttoning her blouse to show him the bruises along her arms and torso from where he'd gripped her. She'd tell him what her friends had said. How sore she was. What she'd been thinking getting drunk alone, missing him, that she'd made a mistake. She wouldn't say thank you. She'd say she knew he still loved her. And because he did, he wouldn't say anything. And when she approached him, he wouldn't move away. And when she placed her lips on his, her hands finding the zipper on his pants, when he felt the tug, if he didn't feel happiness, he'd feel relief.

That would all happen soon.

Tonight, sitting in his car in the parking lot, Pete smoothed a crumpled piece of paper over the steering wheel and wrote the first chords of a bolero.

All the Sex Is West

Inez Suarez didn't have a man, as men who met her liked to ask, or occasionally people at the library where she'd worked since high school, mostly reshelving because she didn't have a degree. Her responses to the men varied from the suspicious, "You think you can be my man?" to the coy, "Who wants to know?" The more honest answer, which she sometimes allowed herself to give to the women at the library, particularly the unattached ones, was something like, "A man? Do they come in faithful?" Because for every time she thought she'd had one, she was proven wrong. Sometimes she felt she'd wiggled her way into their hearts, maneuvering little by little till she was wedged firmly inside, unshakeable. Sometimes the guys were the ones who ran into her arms, grabbing hold hard, begging. Even those always ended up backing away smiling, their hands over their heads—"Later, baby."

No, what Inez Suarez *had* was Los Angeles. And if you had that, men were everywhere. There like rivers and caves and mountains were there. They were places to go—for coolness, for heat, for pleasure, and for business. They were places to visit, to always get back into her car and come back from. Inez had never been further south than Danny in TJ, and no further east than Henry in Las Vegas. She'd once got as far north as Gary in Santa Barbara. She'd taken several excursions to Rick in Newport Beach, where she fell asleep to the lapping of the waves just beyond his bedroom window. None of the guys lasted for very long.

It was the Pacific she came up against again and again, at once stopping her in her tracks and inviting her with its fluid, blue swell to leave her car, her shoes, to be submerged. It was never a perfect invitation, tinged by signs of pollution and cold. But there was no such thing as a perfect invitation. She'd been around enough to know that.

Saturday Night, South El Monte, California

The bodies of mosquitoes floated in Inez Suarez's swimming pool as she walked along the red brick patio, past the hanging plants and shovels with potting soil left out, to her car in the driveway, newly washed at the hand car wash on Peck Road on a day that had been bright blue hot. It was dark now, but the wrought iron chairs and table were still warm to the touch, like the sun had burned itself inside.

Her mother yelled again, louder this time. She was polite and shy with Inez's friends, speaking in the little English she knew. But she always spoke to Inez in Tagalog. She always screamed in Tagalog.

"No. I won't be late." Inez didn't need to raise her voice. Her mother could pick up her slightest vocal sound. Mrs. Suarez yelled again, about vacuuming before the family came, and Inez quickened her pace, her small heels click-clacking on the bricks, and pressed the unlock button on her key chain to save time. She and Andi had run out of her house like this countless times before, fleeing like it was the Temple of Doom and her mother an angry, pierced native who was not sophisticated, who knew nothing of their conquests for glory, discovery, and two-dollar Corona specials. Her pocket felt flat and she almost turned around to retrieve her phone, left recharging in the bathroom. But she could not endanger the mission.

She briefly checked herself in the rearview mirror, moving her bangs over the small bandage on her forehead. Then she pulled out of the driveway, not bothering to close the gate after her, which would earn her more yelling when she got home. Once on Santa Anita, she headed toward the freeway, making a quick stop for a new pack of cigarettes at the Shell station on the corner, and accelerated onto the 60 westbound. It wasn't until she got to that fork of three freeways, sailing right down the middle onto the 101, that she lit a cigarette, inhaled, and blew.

One Week Ago, Somewhere on the 101 Southbound

"Are you sure you're okay?" Andi asked.

Inez was sunken into the passenger seat of her own car, her chin tucked into her chest, just grazing the underside of the seatbelt. She pulled herself upright, slowly so as not to get too dizzy, rubbing her head lightly in assurance. "Sure!"

Andi made a noise. "Why do you always do that?"

"What?"

"You smile with your tongue sticking out. You only do that when you're drunk."

"So what? At least I'm not singing church songs."

"Church songs?"

"Yeah, you always start singing church songs when you're drunk."

"You mean like, there is a balm . . ."

"Stop it."

". . . in Gilead . . ."

"No!" Inez covered her ears. "What's the matter with you? You're not supposed to sing those songs, only in church."

"Why not?" Andi asked, all innocent, and Inez sensed she was teasing her because she was the drunk one, and Andi was not.

"It's sacrilegious," Inez said seriously, annoyed.

"Everything is sacred," Andi replied, stretching out every word, way too happy.

Inez wanted to say "yeah, right," but Andi would read too much into it, so she said, "Turn on the radio."

Andi pushed the knob. There was a commercial, so she went straight to the oldies station. Typical.

Inez called Andi her best friend, though she didn't know if Andi called her that, even when they were in high school, when it would have been obvious. Andi was always slow to say things like that, like she'd have to think about it a lot first. Now, with her away at college except during the summers, Inez really didn't know.

They'd sung in choir together on and off since high school. Andi helped her with her Spanish pronunciation for the special bilingual Masses at Thanksgiving and Christmas. Like she'd helped her get through Spanish class, and every other class. Then Andi came back from college singing in Latin. Songs that freaked Inez out when Andi played the tapes for her, the women's voices so loud they were scary.

Inez watched the road, moving and blurry beneath the headlights. Light from the lampposts poured into the windows in patterns.

"There's a party in Diamond Bar next weekend," Andi said, lowering the volume on the radio. "Maura and I are going."

Diamond Bar was going the wrong way on the 60, and the streets had names like Gunpowder and Lost River. Inez had visited a lot when she was dating Jesse. She stuck out her tongue and made sure not to smile. "No thanks."

"You doing something else?"

Inez touched her head. "I want to go someplace," she said.

Present Day, Sunset Boulevard, Hollywood

Inez ordered a tequila sunrise and plumped herself on a stool at the bar, drinking and grasping her glass with both hands when she wasn't. The seat was empty beside her. A man came up to her. He said he was a chiropractor and started rubbing her back, saying the names of muscles. Trapezius, deltoid. Like those weight machines at the gym with the little charts with the figures on them that said what parts of your body the machine worked out for you. It felt like he was just rubbing hard over her bone. Inez made like she wanted to brush her hair back, moving back his hand.

"Would you be interested in going out with me?" he asked, just like that.

She told him, "No, thank you."

He bowed a little and left her at the bar, sucking through her straw and looking around to see if anyone had noticed her talking to him. Her drink had turned to water.

Upstairs by the dance floor, she ordered another drink to have something to do, and stood by a wooden beam and watched the people dancing to hip hop. It wasn't the kind of music she liked. This tequila sunrise had a green plastic toothpick with a fake cherry and small wedges of lime and lemon. She rotated the toothpick between her fingers, over the mouth of the glass. An older woman came to stand on the other side of the beam, her makeup really caked on, her boobs smashed into a tight top so that her skin puckered in ripples. The woman was standing very close.

One guy asked Inez to dance, and she took his hand. It seemed like he wanted her to get on him, but he didn't pull her close.

"You look bored," he finally said, and she dropped her hand from his shoulder and pushed her way out of the grinding mass.

A half hour till last call, she leaned against a wall downstairs, the exit in sight.

A guy was sitting on a stool by himself, looking out at the crowd. Another night she might have tried making eye contact. Instead, she looked at herself in the mirror, just beyond the assortment of liquors. Big bottles with slender necks. So much glass, so much to smash. Her eyes looked dark, like her makeup was smudging.

She was taking the ice out of her glass, cube by cube, sucking each to obliteration, when another guy walked by her, stopped, and turned back around to face her.

He was barely taller than she was, dark skinned and flushed with heavy eyebrows. His eyes were bright and his smile flitting on and off like a temperamental television set.

"What are you doing?" He looked into her glass and then at her mouth, with the ice cube rolling inside.

"What do you think?"

"Give it to me." He came closer and kissed her. She pushed the ice into his mouth with her tongue.

"Do you want to come home with me? Have a drink?" he asked, and she could hear the ice crunching in his mouth.

"I'm going home."

"Come on. I live really close by." He spoke with an accent. It wasn't Mexican.

"Where are you from?" she asked.

"Israel." The question was still in his eyes. "What happened to your head?"

Inez touched the bandage. "I fell."

"No one was there to catch you?"

"Guess not."

He moved his hand through his hair. "So what do you say? We're good guys." He looked over at the lone guy on the stool, who must have been his friend. But the guy wasn't looking at them.

Before he could push further, he grabbed her shoulder to move out of the way of a busboy. One of his fingers grazed her arm, light and sweet, like a promise.

One Week Ago, a Club on Hollywood Boulevard

Inez stooped on the go-go box, wobbling in her heels. It happened fast. First she was way up high, looking down on everyone, the lights flashing over the tops of their heads. Then her hand was on the cold, hard floor, her hair in her eyes.

"Inez." It was Andi. "Are you all right?" She felt Andi yank her up till the ground pushed up against her feet, painful.

Andi frowned, looking at some space above her eyes. "Shit."

"Shit," Inez repeated. Andi hardly ever swore.

Inez put her hand to her head, and it came away with blood. "They got me."

"Come on." Andi grabbed her around the waist, and they stumbled to the restroom downstairs.

A restroom attendant was sitting by the sink, listening to headphones and reading a paperback. She glanced up at them, then went back to reading.

Andi turned the faucet on and stood behind Inez. "We're gonna clean you up, okay?"

Inez nodded and watched in the mirror as Andi wet a paper napkin and dabbed at her forehead. Then came another towel to pat it dry, and from somewhere, two Band-Aids to cover the cut.

A little blood had splattered onto Inez's chest, and Andi wet another napkin and rubbed it over her harder, having to wipe a little into her cleavage to get it all.

"Woo," Inez said, puffing out her chest.

"All right, all right."

A drop of water ran down her chest, and she felt it move between her breasts, unbelievably slowly.

"Hold still," Andi told her.

Some girls walked in laughing, then stopped at seeing Inez. "Is she all right?"

"Yeah." Andi put her arm around Inez's shoulders. "She's just been wounded in battle. Huh, Nez?"

"Oh," the girls said and looked at each other, like Andi and Inez were both weirdos. Inez wanted to tell them to get lost, but Andi turned her around and inspected her, looking into her eyes. "Okay. I think you're not bleeding anymore."

"That's what you think," Inez said automatically, like she would do when joking around, wanting to disagree with whatever Andi said. But the words hit her afterward and her eyes stung.

A stall door swung open, and a girl came out slowly, gripping the side of the door, her eyes puffy and red. Andi still had Inez by the shoulders, ready to walk her out, but Inez resisted her pull long enough to ask the girl, "Hey, having fun?"

Back upstairs, Andi steering her toward the exit, she tried scanning the room, looking for the spot where she fell.

Present Day, a Club on Sunset Boulevard

His friend was named David, and he was Adán. Adán walked with Inez to her car. David would drive theirs home. It was 2 A.M., and the guts of Sunset were spilling out, all the cars and people reeling into the open spaces, crazily because they'd been back-to-back in the clubs and double-parked in the lots. The tequila had put a nice haze over everything, but Inez drove steadily, used to it.

Adán leaned back in the seat like it was the most comfortable place in the world, like he'd always been there. "So who are you coming to be with? Me or my roommate? Make a left here."

She chanced a glance at him in the middle of the intersection. "What do you mean?"

"You know, cuz there are two of us."

"I know, but—"

"Pull in here."

The apartment was close, just like he'd said. They pulled into an alley and parked alongside the building. She followed Adán to a black iron gate. "David's got the key." She wanted to ask him what he'd meant in the car about his roommate, but a homeless man was walking toward them. All the cars were behind fences under the apartments—it looked like he was staying in one of them. "Can I come inside?" the man asked. "I gotta use the toilet."

Adán didn't answer, just watched David as he came walking up from the other side. He had parked on the street.

"Will my car be okay here?" Inez asked. "There are signs." She thumbed at a prominent NO PARKING sign on the wall.

"It doesn't matter at this time. Come on, David, let us in."

David got to the gate, and the two of them stood murmuring. The homeless man addressed Inez. "Do you act or sing?" he asked, as though she had to do either one or the other.

She looked to the guys, but they weren't paying attention. "I used to sing in a choir."

"Come find me later. I'm a producer. I produce all kinds of acts."

"Okay."

"I'll be right over there." He pointed at some trashcans. "Come and find me."

The gate swung open. "Good night," David told the man, and the three of them went inside.

Once in the apartment, David went right to his room.

Adán took her hand and pulled her to a couch and kissed her neck.

"Do you know that man?"

"Yes. He sleeps right outside our window sometimes. We give him fruit."

Adán stood up and took off his pants. With his hand on her head, he pushed her down toward him. She resisted a second, but only a second.

Once she had made him come, he asked her to do it again.

"But you just came," she said. Maybe he was really drunk.

"But it feels so good. You can do it again." His eyes were still dancing, not in rhythm now that they were out of the club.

She sat back in reply, and smoothed the edges of the bandage on her head. The doctor had given her something thicker than a Band-Aid, and gauze. She would be all right. But she had a gash, a neat little arc, precise, like she'd meant it.

Adán pulled his boxers back on and lit a cigarette, looking perfectly content. She thought about touching his leg. But he didn't look at her, so she folded her arms up into her chest. Her contacts were feeling dry, heavy on her eyes, and she blinked deliberately.

"What were you doing there tonight?" he asked.

"What do you mean?"

"At the club, alone. What were you looking for?"

She shrugged, starting to wonder if she shouldn't have come home with him. "I don't know."

"Were you looking for this?"

She looked around the room. There were two full ashtrays on the table and magazines and clothes all over the place. The couch felt too porous almost, like it would suck her up if she wasn't careful. "I guess I was looking for something more."

His eyes widened. "You mean, full-on sex?"

"Not that kind of more."

They both laughed.

"Come on." He stood up and took her hand, leading her to a bedroom.

At the bed, he started kissing her. She turned her head. "Should I close the door?"

"Should I call my roommate over?" he parroted her, his eyebrows wagging.

"What? No."

He called out in Hebrew. Inez didn't understand what he'd said. Maybe it was an enchantment, because then David appeared behind her, kissing her shoulder. It stunned her how fast he was there, and how focused he was on her. He kissed her neck, her jaw. When his lips released her skin, the air swooped in, tingling her.

They led her down onto the bed. David kissed her, playing with her tongue lightly, then plunging his deep inside her mouth. Her shoes came off, then her skirt. She couldn't see him, but she could feel Adán, one of his hands on the top of her thigh, pressing her into the bed, the other rubbing over the cotton of her panties. David grabbed both her hands and held them above her head, against the wooden headboard. His other hand was under her shirt, moving over her breast. Adán kept moving over her panties, just rubbing up and down in a regular motion. When his fingers moved under the fabric, she felt the instant tingle and the heat shot to the bottoms of her feet. David kept his mouth clamped firmly over hers, not kissing anymore or moving his tongue, just holding her. She could feel the open space, a tunnel of wind inside him giving her breath, and when the time came she cried out with his mouth still over hers, her voice loud in her own ears.

David released her mouth and hands when she stopped trembling.

The pressure lifted from her pelvis and she felt the bed rise. Adán had left the room.

The television in the living room blared on, and Adán yelled out something in that other language. David laughed apologetically. "My roommate is crazy. It's just us now," he whispered, smoothing back her hair. She was still trying to catch her breath, her heart pounding in her chest.

"Come on," he said. "Let's go to my room. He might want to sleep." She grabbed her skirt and shoes from the floor, and he led her by the hand out to the hallway and into his room. He closed the door behind them.

They stripped to their underwear and got under the covers. His body lean and muscular, she nestled against him, and they lay just like that, only their fingers moving, to rub an arm, or scratch the base of a neck.

"You look a little like a girl I know in Israel."

"Really?"

He smiled. "Mostly your mouth. What are you?"

Inez got this question a lot, usually from foreign men. "*I am from here. My parents are from the Philippines.*"

"Have you ever been to Israel?"

"No. What part are you from?" She wouldn't have known one part from another, but it seemed the polite thing to ask.

He leaned over the edge of the bed and retrieved a pen. He wasn't finding paper, so she offered him her hand. They turned onto their stomachs, and soon the country was centered on her palm.

David had made little dots for cities and ovals for bodies of water. "I live up here, right? And I work here, in Jerusalem. This is where all our water supply comes from. All these countries that border get their water from here. And this is where the fighting is." He made little undefined squiggles in numerous regions for this. When he was done, he took her hand in both of his and rubbed at the ink lines. He licked his finger and rubbed with the saliva, but the lines stayed.

"I have a condom," he said, his eyes still downcast. She could see the full length of his lashes.

"That's all right."

"You don't want to have sex?"

"I have this policy of not having it."

"Are you a virgin?" he asked.

"Well, technically."

He grinned. "What does that mean, 'technically'?"

"You know."

He shook his head. "No, I don't."

"It means I've done stuff. Just not *it* exactly." She punched him playfully in the shoulder for having to spell it out.

"Oh, I see. How old are you anyway?" he asked.

"Twenty-two."

David frowned. "That's not common, is it, in this country? To be, technically?"

She shrugged. "I guess not."

"You've never wanted to? Not even in the passion of the moment?"

"The passion of the moment?" It was an almost funny overstatement of the present one.

"Yes, you don't lose yourself?"

Guys had asked her this before, in one way or another, and she always had the sense that what they were talking about was something real, but not passion exactly.

David flipped onto his back and put his arms underneath his head. "Maybe I'm not saying the right thing."

"No, you're fine." She stretched to kiss his cheek and felt the whole length of her body along the white linen sheets.

There wasn't the sound of water or crickets here, or even street noise. She heard steps echoing in the alley, then a dog barking, then nothing. She closed her eyes, her face close to David's warm skin, so close that she could feel her own breath blowing back on her.

Ongoing, Hollywood

Hollywood was both her and Andi's first love. The minute Inez turned eighteen, they started hitting up the clubs, searching out Brit-pop and soul and '80s music. It wasn't long until they'd developed a set of rituals involving sneaky drinking in the car, one gulping and the other keeping an eye out for security guards, and late-night feasts of either Thai or bacon-wrapped hotdogs off the street.

The clubs had a certain feel, an undertone of something old and grand, all blends of red velvet, dark wood, and chandeliers. The night began with just a few people on the dance floor, the lights moving over them. Andi and Inez would get their first drinks, take them to the dance floor and sway and step, cool and upright. More people would come, and they would eventually find themselves surrounded. Singing to Bowie, The Cure, Madonna. Dirty lyrics with little-girl beats. Inez shouted out every word. They'd stop drinking at some point, to have both hands free. And it's then they could let loose and rage all they wanted. With less space, Inez had to reign in her movements, her motions more focused. But no matter how full it got, it never got too full. She could stretch her hand out on either side of Andi's head, over her own, step and kick and jump. She could whip her hair around, feel it soft on her face. Move forward and back, in the small space around her, the space that was hers no matter how close anyone else got. In and out, like breathing. They weren't like other girls they had known, who thought grinding and faux lesbian dancing counted. They were following the fastest beat, having to tie their hair up for the sweat on their necks. Pounding their feet into the ground, without mercy, able to do this until they left the club, and then, like a wand had been tapped, each step so painful that they'd hobble, howling like monkeys, back to the car.

They'd invited other girls out dancing, girls with boyfriends, girls between boyfriends. Girls always searching the crowd or checking their pagers or going to stand by the bar. Inez and Andi went to meet guys, too, of course. Alternative Mexican boys with spiky gelled hair, dressed all in black, embarrassingly gentle. Groping white boys with blue eyes and indie band T-shirts. Inez liked their hands on her waist, her hips, liked their chests pressed against her back, their thighs under her hand.

But they always slowed her down. It was only before the guys found her, when she was still on her own, that she wasn't wanting or hoping or waiting for anything to come. The world could pass away right then and it would be fine.

Present Day, Early Sunday Morning, Somewhere off Fountain

Inez knew to leave when the sky got lighter.

David gathered up her clothes and left her to dress while he used the bathroom. She zipped up her skirt and buckled her shoes, alone in his room with his things.

The door to Adán's room was shut and the television turned off in the living room. David walked her out the door to the patio. He took her hand and added his phone number to the map. "You are always welcome here. You don't have to call. Just stop by whenever you want."

She laughed. "Yeah, I'll pay another visit to you and Adán."

"No, I mean it. For whatever reason, if you want to come, you are welcome."

"Thanks." They pecked on the lips, like a couple. Inez couldn't remember ever having done that before.

He held open the gate for her, then went back inside the apartment, looking at the ground when he closed the door. The alley was still. Inez looked for the man who said he was a producer, but he was nowhere. A hum filled her throat, a vibrating. "There is . . . a balm . . ." In the car, the first thing she did was find her lavender-scented lotion and rub it over her hands. She rubbed at the map and phone number with a tissue until they were gone.

The car responded to her touch with its sweet mechanical sounds. Music up, windows down, sunroof open. Back on the freeway, the sun shone in her eyes. The first sunlight always felt different. It was just entering the world, new. Inez slipped her sunglasses off the visor, shook them open, and slid them onto her ears. Leaning back into the seat, her left leg up on the car door, the leather wheel warm against the inside of her knee, her right hand steered loosely against her thigh. Just before the 101 fed into the 60, the car jostled at that one point where the road was uneven. Inez prepared for the familiar bounce, checking her blind spot, then moving into that new lane that was as big as two, her foot pressing harder on the gas as the white lines narrowed to hug her.

With hardly any traffic, she was soon at the Santa Anita exit. She drove over the bridge bordered by chain-link fences, the signs of the Ramada, Mobil, and Burger King growing from their stems, until the car reached the crest, and she eased her foot off the gas pedal, coasting into the outstretched street.

Happy Hour

T he bar's ceiling is painted in thick, black swirls. It's low, with orna-
ments hanging by short ribbons. In the far corner on a ledge is a small
statue of Mary, a bouquet of fabric roses at her feet. White Christmas
lights are draped over her, blinking.

The place is empty so we have our pick of stools. Dad's still wearing
his suit from the morning, though he's taken off the jacket and tie. We
don't have to wait long for the bartender.

"Hey, Tony. Where you been?" She comes out from a door in the
back. She is petite and looks Mexican. She's wearing a tiger-striped hal-
ter and her hair's teased out like in an '80s music video. A cross on a
gold chain is peeking out of her cleavage.

"Hi, Rita."

I haven't heard anyone call Dad "Tony" in forever. The scattered
girlfriends he's had always call him "Anthony"—I'm not sure why. And
Mom just calls him "your dad," when she calls him anything.

"Just got back from my mother's funeral," Dad tells her.

"Oh, I'm sorry!"

"This is my daughter, Maura."

"Really!" Rita's sympathetic face turns into a happy one.

"Half Mexican, half Irish," Dad says.

Rita nods and folds her arms over her chest, "Very good," like Dad's just taken up the glasses on the bar and juggled them for her. Me and Andi would always get people asking us how we were sisters, like it was a physical impossibility. She looked Mexican, and a lot like Mom. I didn't really look like anybody, but I had blond hair and blue eyes. It was always the people I liked most who could see similarities between us. In our expressions and our voices. Our eyes, though different in color, were the same shape.

"We'll have two Coronas," Dad says.

"Sure, Tony." Rita turns to pull two beers out of a fridge by her knees.

"I knew that if I didn't say anything, they'd think you were my date or something," Dad tells me.

He improvises the gossip and I laugh.

"'He's old enough to be her father!'"

Rita returns. She sets two napkins on the bar and puts the bottles down.

"You want a lime, honey?"

"Yes, please," I say. She doesn't ask Dad, and inserts the wedge into my bottle. I pull it out and squeeze the lime above the opening, the juice and bits running down the sides of the bottle. Then I push the slice of lime down the neck, sucking the juice off my thumb.

"I brought Andi here once," Dad says. "They won't check ID cuz you're with me. But it's more believable with you, that you're my daughter, I mean."

If someone were to look at my ID, they'd see the only indication of anything Spanish about me. They'd see my name "Maura," for my grandma, Moira, and "Rowe," my Dad's name. And there in the middle they'd see "Guadalupe." I used to think it a very ugly name. Too long, too serious. A mouthful.

Mom got to pick our middle names, and she chose appearances of Mary for both of us, Andi getting "Lourdes." When we were in junior high and making up aka's, renaming ourselves every week, in one scenario we would be Lulu and Lupe. And we'd even write stories about the adventures of Lulu and Lupe, like they were our secret identities. I think that I'll be Lupe when I go to South America for a semester next year. I'll just tell everyone that's my name.

Grandma looked different in the casket last night. Thinner, paler. Which isn't strange, I know. But her hair surprised me. She'd been dyeing it pale blond for years, and it had turned completely white since the last time I'd seen her. As a kid, I had thought I inherited my blond hair from her. Dad didn't have it, after all. But Grandma had actually had dark brown hair, almost black. I saw it in the Polaroids in the photo albums Mom kept. Grandma with her dark hair in a beehive, smoking, in a shift dress. And later, in the old home movies our one uncle had kept. I loved those old movies, silent, with their halting motions. The people looked so cheerful and frank, like out of an old sitcom. I was disappointed about Grandma's hair though. It felt like I'd lied to the people who asked about my hair. I was actually kind of angry about it. Looking back, I think it was more about not having an easy answer anymore. The truth was much more convoluted. I did get her blue eyes. But I couldn't see those at the rosary.

It was a long drive back from Fresno, me and Dad not talking much. We mostly just listened to Bob Dylan as we drove though the mountains and along the grapevine, eating strawberries we'd bought at a fruit stand out of the green foam carton between us. It was so foggy up in the mountains, we had to crawl along at a few points.

When we stopped for gas, I borrowed Dad's cell phone to call the house, to ask how Mom was. It had taken her some time to settle down, Andi said, but she'd finally fallen asleep on the drive back. She was resting. Crying, but calm.

"You don't have to rush back. Take care of Dad," Andi said.

And even though Mom was a mess at the funeral and it was scary even, taking care of Dad seems like the taller order. With Mom I could make herbal tea and rub her back, and we could watch one of those cheesy movies she likes.

But Dad—who knows what he needs now or what he's ever needed. All I can do is just be with him. I've been with him all weekend. Entering the rosary last night, with the viewing, I saw Mom and Andi across the church. I just waved over at them and they waved back. It was like I couldn't walk from Dad to them. And they didn't cross over either.

"So your grandma's gone," Dad says after his first drink of beer. "You never be mean to your mother. Cuz she's the one who gave you life." He says it like Grandma gave birth to him and then promptly left him on a doorstep somewhere.

Rita plops a bowl of chips and a little glass dish of salsa on the bar and winks at us. She sashays back behind a door. I take a chip. They're surprisingly thick. Like someone cut up the tortilla strips themselves and fried them in oil, hand sprinkled them with salt. The salsa isn't bad either, though it's mild. Something about the chips and salsa and the plop and wink tell me we're getting special treatment. Dad takes a chip and scoops some salsa, slanting his head to fit the chip in his mouth and crunching loudly.

"Everyone's dying," he continues. "This guy who lived down the hall from me. The only guy I talked to, really." He took a drink. "They found him last week in his room. They figured he'd been dead a few days. They only went in there to collect the rent. That guy, he drank like a case of beer and a bottle of liquor every day. He was almost as bad as that Kerouac. You can't live long when you're drinking like that."

"No," I agree.

"Now there's a guy who did too much drugs." Dad gestures to the juke box. The Doors are playing.

We're into one of Dad's favorite subjects now. While other people may be obsessed with celebrity marriages and breakups, Dad has always been interested in celebrity deaths. Actors, writers, musicians—it doesn't matter. He can rattle off the age and cause. He always ends up comparing them to himself. He still has his health. Each day he's getting stronger, one of the fittest. And this isn't a recent thing because he's getting older. He's always been this way, for as far back as I can remember.

"And I'd seen him the week before," Dad says. "He walked by me in the hall. There was this awful smell, and I didn't realize what it was until I went into my room. It was him. He was actually rotting from the inside." Dad cups his hands at his chest, to signify this. "At that point, you know there's nothing you can do."

Just thinking of Dad smelling this dying man makes me cringe. I imagine him in the crappy apartment complex up the street that he's been living in for the past few months, ever since he got back from Vegas. I take another swallow of beer. Not knowing what else to say, it seems the only appropriate thing to do is to add to the list of the deceased. "My mom's uncle, Tío Francisco, died this spring. He had cancer."

"Oh, yeah, Francisco," Dad says, suddenly energized. "He was a nice guy. We used to go over to his house in Highland Park for parties. No one cared how you danced, it was just to have fun. I tell you, you go to these white people's parties, and it's completely different."

He doesn't say how, and he doesn't have to. I make the leap.

"That's why I always liked those Latin girls, with the big Mexican families. It's like your Mom today. No one else was crying, and it's their own mother."

I saw Aunt Peggy tearing up, but I don't correct him.

"I at least squeezed out a few drops. But your mom, that was impressive."

Impressive isn't the word I would have used, and I've never seen Dad cry, not ever. "I hope she's okay," I say.

"Mexicans are much freer about their feelings. Not like white people. But you and Andi, you've got the best of both worlds."

I smile. I don't say it's always been just the one world split.

I didn't cry as much as I thought I would. Grandma's the first person close to me who has died. But I never was much of a crier. Years ago, closer to the divorce I guess, Mom would sometimes come home from work, collapse on the couch and without a word just start crying. We never knew why exactly. Well, we did and we didn't. It was all so big and sad that articulating it would have seemed somehow too obvious. And when Mom got like that, Andi would cry with her. Just like that, without Mom even having to say anything. Mom just breathing and sighing, so helpless when I think about it. So helpless that it scared me and made me mad to see her like that. And I would sit with them through it all because I had to. But I wouldn't cry.

If Dad started to cry now, I don't know what I'd do. But he seems okay. It's kind of nice to be in this dingy bar with him, listening to all the strange explanations he comes up with. It's always so black and white with him. "Thanks, by the way, for back at the house," I say.

"Dan has always been an idiot. Some people just don't have any brains. It was obvious she was upset. And they're trying to pull her into the house, like that'll make things better. It's this silly logic of 'you need to lie down or sit down.' The whole problem is the place. It's psychological."

It was like a movie or something back at Grandma's house after the funeral this morning. Seeing Dad appear in the doorway as they were trying to pull Mom, sobbing, inside. She had been walking toward the house and then she just stopped, started shaking her hand like she had a cramp, holding her head, breathing really deep. She was just stopped there in the driveway, inhaling and exhaling, like she couldn't take another step. Like the ground had opened up and she was standing on the edge of a cliff. Andi told me she'd been freaking out on the way over. Saying that Grandma wouldn't be here. She wouldn't be here to greet us. People were grabbing her, and me and Andi didn't know what to do. Dad told them to let her go.

Even when Uncle Dan told Dad it wasn't his business, Dad still wouldn't move. And that's when we got a hold of Mom and steered her back to the car, away from Grandma's empty house. She'd been okay at the rosary and the cemetery. The house was just too much, I guess.

Our original travel plans had been to switch off, so we could each spend time with Dad. But when Mom freaked out, we wanted to get her home as soon as possible. I hadn't even packed my luggage yet. Mom and Andi were gonna miss the whole reception.

"Your mom and my mom were really close," Dad says.

He's never talked about Mom as much as he is now. It feels like something is changing, something key. I'm glad that he saw it, too, that Mom and Grandma were crazy about each other. They had a lot in common. They were both immigrants, Grandma leaving Ireland for the U.K. and then coming to the U.S. once she got married. They were both ardent Catholics and started working at an early age. Both left by their husbands, for one reason or another.

"You know, your mom didn't really have a mother. Just that awful Abuelita."

I have to smile at the ridiculous drawn out way he says the Spanish word. He knows better of course, not that he ever learned Spanish.

"Want to pick a song for us?" he asks me.

"Sure."

He gives me a quarter.

I flip through a few of the pages in the jukebox. I pick a Bob Dylan song, deliberately. Good ole Bob will be sixty this year. Andi and I had a Bob Dylan party once, when Mom was away visiting relatives in Mexico. We baked a cake and iced it in vanilla frosting, and Andi used cut Peppermint Patties for Bob's glasses and broken up pretzels for his hair. We made drinks we called "Texas medicine" and "railroad gin," and it all reminded me of him, somehow. Of Dad, because he's the one who played Bob for us. We should have invited him, but of course we never could.

Dad picks up his empty bottle and points to mine with a free finger. I finish it.

"That woman hated me, I'll tell you that," Dad says, and I realize he's still thinking of Abuelita. He chuckles, as if fond memories of the angry, old Mexican lady are running through his mind. It's strange, like it's a source of comfort, her disapproval of him.

Abuelita died several years ago in the back room of our house, Mom caring for her. Mom lit a candle for her when she died and added her name to the list she keeps tucked in her Bible by her bed. She keeps a list of all the dead family members so she can remember to pray for them. Her parents are on it, Dad's father. Maybe everyone is morbid in their own way. Maybe you have to be so you don't forget.

"I have no more grandparents," I say.

"Well, I'm an orphan," Dad says, topping me. There's a softness in his eyes. We have to laugh because it's pretty silly, the idea of this graying, middle-aged orphan. "Be happy you're not an orphan, Maura. Not yet anyway."

Outside is Los Angeles Harbor, and the air smells like fish. Dad used to take us to the port before he even lived here. We'd go to the Shakespeare by the Sea Festival during the summers, eat salty fish wrapped in newspaper. San Pedro always reminded me of San Francisco—the nearby water that wasn't a beach, the hilly streets. It was a place separate from the rest of Los Angeles.

I drop Dad off in the parking lot of his apartment complex, and he gets out of the car and looks in to give a little wave of good-bye. I know I should go out to hug him. It suddenly feels so sad to be sitting behind the steering wheel, him stooping to look in. But just thinking about all this makes it harder for me to move.

"Thanks for the ride, Maura."

"No problem."

"Love you."

"Love you," I say back. We always leave out the *I*s. I like it that way. Then it sounds like this love comes from the wider world, and it's not all on me to make him feel it, to make him believe, so that he knows I do.

Dad shuts the door too lightly and has to open it again to close it better.

I pull back into the street where I'm stuck waiting on a red. The seconds tick by and still the light doesn't change. He has walked up the stairs and is standing by the railing. He usually waits to go inside until I'm out of sight. I look in my rear view mirror and wave to him. He waves back.

Suddenly, Bob's harmonica sounds really loud in the car, and I jump, my heart racing. My hand darts for the dial to turn it down, and I move my hair out of my face. It's an old car. Andi's from high school, a used Toyota. Its speakers don't work so well. Sometimes I'll be driving and the sound kicks in, and I'll realize that I hadn't noticed it was lowered for all that time.

There's a laminated prayer card from the rosary on the floor. Dad must have left it. The front has a picture of Mary. On the back it says, Moira Agatha Rowe, and what must be an Irish prayer. "Let my name be ever the household word it always was / Let it be spoken without effort."

I take a deep breath. I'm going home to Mom and Andi, to the neighborhood I grew up in, to the house Dad bought for him and Mom, before he'd ever met me, before I was born. I'm going back to my life. Dad gave this to me, not in the way that Mom did, maybe. He gave it to me just by wanting it for himself, if only for awhile.

I think of Grandma, alive with blond hair. I think if I pronounce my name "Mao-ra" when I'm in Chile, it should be easy enough for people to say.

The light turns green, and I move forward. Dad's still standing at the top of the stairs, getting very small in the mirror. It's then that I start to cry.

The Body

When Father Felipe says we're celebrating the feast of Corpus Christi, at first I think, why are we celebrating some lame city in Texas? But then he says it means the Body of Christ, and I think, oh, shit, I should've known that. Maybe Mom was right and all that Catholic school *was* a waste. All I know is that I'm glad it's Sunday. I had to get out of there. Church is the only place Mom will let me go when I'm in trouble or grounded. The problem is, I don't even know if I'm in trouble.

When I got here, I went to sit in the back pew. Like Maria and I always do. Maria's not here today though. Maybe that's why Ms. Rowe came up to me. All the times I've come, she's never asked me to serve before. It sucks they're short a person. Ms. Rowe is funny though. During confirmation class, too, she never told anyone to do anything. She always asked. Teresa, would you like to start us off? Teresa, do you want to read this passage? And she was so nice, you couldn't say no. Even though after awhile that's all you wanted to say, really loud. No, I don't want to think of a time I turned to God! But I guess it's better than Mom, saying she asked me to do something and getting mad, when she never asked me to do anything.

So I said, yeah, whatever and Ms. Rowe got all happy and said, wonderful! Everything's wonderful with her. Then she sat down and told me what I had to do. Like I haven't been to Mass a trillion times before. But she wanted me to be sure when to go up, where everyone else would be. It made me think of the Powder Puff game last year, where the captain took out a paper and made Xs for the players and drew arrows everywhere about where we should run. Kind of unnecessary. Amanda wouldn't pass the ball just because the diagram said she would. Ms. Rowe invited me to sit up front with her, but I said no thank you! I don't like sitting in the front. I feel like everyone's watching me. And maybe Maria will show up after all. Although, maybe that would make me more nervous, now that I have to serve communion. She wasn't here last Sunday either. I wonder if she's going to a different Mass. The Spanish one? Or maybe she's just not going at all. Last week was the Holy Trinity Mass. I remember because there were three little boys sitting in front of me, and they were cute and all around the same size, which was weird. I wish Maria would come, even if she would laugh at me.

I met Maria in seventh grade, when I started Catholic school. Even then, everyone loved her. You just couldn't help it. Even the white teachers who were just out of college drooled over her. Maria's pretty and speaks Spanish and tells funny stories about her and her mom making tamales. They eat that shit up. That's how I know they came to teach Mexican girls like her. Not like me, who don't know Spanish. Mom's meals come out of cans, mostly. It doesn't make for such a great story.

I never told my mom how the girls do stuff to each other at our school. They don't think it counts, cuz you can't get pregnant. Definitely, if it weren't for Maria, none of this would have happened. She promised we were best friends who told each other everything, and then she won't talk to me one day. She just won't. Someone's been talking shit about me. Ever since that party. Mom probably thinks now that I met Dominic there. But there were never any guys there. It was girls, always girls. Mom never let me go out on the weekend. I don't know why she did that time. I thought it was gonna be cool. So stupid. I knew what they did at those slumber parties. Girls kissed each other, or worse. Not because they really wanted to, but because everyone was doing it. But Maria was going. I wanted to see what she would do. I didn't wanna play the game they were playing, and Desiree said it was because I was a lesbian. No one had ever called me that before. And that made me mad. Because I'd never done anything with a girl. Nothing ever, I swear to God! But everyone was laughing at me, calling me a lesbo. What bullshit! I thought Maria would defend me, but I saw her in the corner. She had her hand over her face. She was trying not to laugh.

After that, Maria was really quiet around me. She went out with Danny Ramirez, and she wouldn't even tell me about it when I asked her. So I said fine and I left. I met Dominic at a retreat. I was only gonna be with him for a little while. To see what it was like. Show Maria that I could get a boy, too, if I wanted. Now I'm kinda hoping Mom does pull me out and sends me to South El Monte. I wanna be away from all that. She thinks as long as I'm with the church people, nothing bad will happen. But she doesn't even go anymore. How would she know?

Father's giving his sermon now, talking about some Vietnamese bishop in prison who said Mass by putting drops of wine on his palm and how they had to change guards on him because he kept converting them cuz he was so nice. I try to concentrate cuz it's getting closer to when I have to go up. I wish Ms. Rowe was with me. She said I'd be doing the Body. I guess that's okay. I'd be afraid to spill the wine. And you gotta wipe the cup each time someone drinks. With the Body though, you gotta deal with the tongue. Cuz that's where some people want it. I hope I don't end up touching anyone's slimy tongue on accident. Gross! Also, I'll probably get more people. Cuz a lot don't take the wine. They just take the Body and go. I'm not sure which is better. Maybe when I get there, one of the ladies will want to trade.

I raise my hands for the Our Father, cuz that's how I learned how to pray it. We used to hold each other's hands. It seems so long ago! But I guess they think this way is better now. I tell the people in front peace be with them and shake their hands. Ms. Rowe is way at the front, waiting for me to make it down the aisle. People look at me. I get there and try to bow at the same time she does. Then I follow her over to the side of the altar where we're supposed to stand. Here's the part I'm not so sure about.

Father holds up the host, and the altar server girl rings a bell. He puts it down, then he holds up the wine, and the girl rings the bell again. He puts the cup down.

Father turns to the side and gives us all the Body. Then he gives the

Blood to Ms. Rowe and some other lady, and they take the chalices. Ms. Rowe holds the cup out to me and says, "Blood of Christ." I say, "Amen" and take the cup and just sip. I give it back to her, and she tells me to get the dish of hosts from the altar. Father goes to stand toward the left side, so I go to the right. People start walking up.

The choir comes up first, and I'm on their side, so they come to me. I know Pete and Gabe from the youth group. They smile at me when they see me. They're older, but I think they're friends with Dominic. They don't seem like they know anything about what's going on. Dominic would probably get in trouble if they knew. I'm not gonna say anything about him. But I could if I wanted to. When Dominic kisses me, I feel like I'm not there. I feel him on my lips. I feel everything he's doing, but I'm away from it somehow. Away from my body, like it's not really me. Like I'm somewhere else, watching it happen. It's kind of nice that way.

"The Body of Christ." An old guy gets down on one knee and crosses himself like a lot of the old people do. "The Body of Christ." This woman moves her mouth amen, but no words come out. She takes the host without looking at me.

When I was little, I didn't want to chew it cuz I was afraid of hurting Jesus with my teeth. Can you believe it?

Father hasn't turned off his microphone, and we can all hear him. "The Body of Christ." "The Body of Christ." "The Body of Christ." "The Body of Christ." Jesus!

"The Body of Christ." A little girl comes up and I wonder if she's even old enough, but she looks like she knows what she's doing. She holds her hands up in front of her forehead, and I place the host in her palm.

Now I like to chew on the host. It feels good eating it, and I wish I'd started sooner.

All the people look different. Some of the moms are holding babies or the hands of little kids. Some are real serious but some smile, and some look me in the eye and some don't at all. And some put the host in their mouths in front of me, but most turn away to do it while they're walking, and some bow after.

The last man comes up. The music has stopped already, and it's like everyone's watching me. He sticks out his tongue, and I've got the hang of it now. I put it on the front of his tongue, without touching it. Take that!

Ms. Rowe comes to take my dish, and she gives me her chalice. She gets all the hosts together and I follow her to the tabernacle. I wait while she puts the leftover Body away and locks the little gold door. Then we go into the sacristy.

She says we gotta finish the wine and do I want to do it. Okay!

I get all the Blood in one swallow. Man! Ms. Rowe tells me to set the chalice on the counter, and we go back out to the church. Instead of walking all the way to the back, I sit with her.

It's pretty near the end now. A woman makes the announcements and reminds us to take the bulletin home. I need to get one for Mom. She still likes to read it, even though she doesn't go to Mass anymore.

Father Felipe says that for anyone who wants, the Blessed Sacrament will be on display in the monstrance. The monstrance? We should please sign up to spend a half hour with the Eucharist. He waves over to the right, by Mary. There's like a big, gold candlestick, but with a round center, just big enough for the host. Gold spikes and zigzags are coming out of it, like they come out of Mary.

Father says that the Mass has ended, to go in peace. We say thanks be to God, which has always sounded funny to me cuz it sounds like we're saying we're glad to be outta there. Ms. Rowe has her songbook open and is singing in her high voice that doesn't sound totally right, and I don't want to go home so I stay with her. At the end of the song, people clap for the choir. I hope Pete and Gabe don't come over. I don't really feel like talking to them.

Ms. Rowe puts her hand on my shoulder and asks if I want her to show me how to clean up. Here we go again.

We go back to the sacristy. The glasses and bowls are set by the sink. There's a clipboard for where the Eucharistic ministers are supposed to sign in, and I ask her if I should sign in or if it's too late, and she says, sure, honey. I sign my name Teresa Maldonado, with stars for the Os, and now I'm in the book!

Ms. Rowe starts rinsing things under the faucet and places them on the counter. She gives me a small, white cloth to dry them with. It's not like a dishcloth, which is made for that stuff, but it's okay. She says that for all the ones that had the bread or the wine in 'em, they wash them in the right part of the sink. Cuz that one leads to the earth, and the other one to the sewer.

She asks me to see which cups had the wine, and I pick one up. Yup. That's booze smell.

We gotta purify 'em, she says. And I think, is she talking about a fire? So I ask and she's like what are you talking about and I say, do we gotta heat 'em up or something and she says oh no, I'll show you.

I'm embarrassed I got it wrong, but she doesn't care. She fills the cup with some water from the faucet and starts moving it around like they do on TV when they have a glass of wine they're getting ready to smell and drink.

She says we're gonna do that for all the glasses, pouring the water into one after the other. And then with the last cup you drink all the tap water. So I do that. I go through all the cups. And I drink the water from the last one and set it down. That's it I ask her and she's like that's it, they're purified!

Okay. It doesn't seem like we really washed them. But all right.

She gives me a white cloth to dry them. She calls the cloth the purificator, and I start laughing cuz I'm imagining it's the terminator of napkins. She asks what I'm laughing about and I tell her, and Ms. Rowe does an impression. What the fuck?! We're both laughing like crazy in the fucking sacristy. I guess Mass is over, but damn. They're never gonna let me back here again.

I haven't eaten, and I can feel the wine in my stomach. It gives off like little warm punches. The only wine I've ever had besides Communion was at a party once, and it made me sick. But I drank too much.

One of the other women starts talking to Ms. Rowe, so I walk back over to the clipboard where I signed my name. There's another one by it, and it says it's for Adoration.

Ms. Rowe says we're done, and I ask if I can get a ride home. I don't know why. I could walk, but I don't feel like it. It's hot outside. Ms. Rowe says sure, but she's gotta pray first cuz she signed up to do Adoration for a half hour. This lady! She wants me to pray with her, but I don't feel like it so I tell her, nah, I'll wait for her. I walk outside to wait on a bench. There are some people. And Father's out there, talking. I remember when they put in these tiles in front of the church. It wasn't that long ago, really. Well, I was going to elementary school here. I sit on a bench with the plants behind me. One of the plants is itching me, so I gotta move over.

Last night Dominic picked me up and took me to the back of the community center where it was dark, and we could do it in the car. I didn't stop him. I never stop him, because you don't do that if you like boys. You let them touch you. I tried to break up with him after, but it's like he wouldn't let me. He kept saying, but I love you so much, baby. I have to be with you. Jesus! I kept telling him to take me home, I was gonna be late. But he wouldn't! By the time I got there, it was really late. I tried sneaking in, but Mom caught me coming. Who were you with? She starts screaming at me, crazy. She's so angry! Ay no one I tell her. I don't wanna say, I don't know why. Who was it? Who *pendeja* she calls me. Just some guy I say, and I'm crying by that time. So she stops scream-ing finally and tells me to go to bed. I ask her am I in trouble. She just says go to bed. So I go to my room and change. I sit on the bed, waiting for her to come in and yell more, maybe even hit me. I don't want to be laying in bed when she comes in. I can picture her throwing herself on top of me like a crazy woman. Once I got home late in eighth grade. I said I'd be back in time for dinner. She went psycho on me. I was grounded for a month. No phone, no friends, no TV. I was never late again. But I'd never done anything this bad, not ever. And I wondered if she could see it in my face what I'd done. I was there forever, it felt like, just sitting on my bed, my heart beating really fast, watching the door. But all the lights went out, and then the door to her room closed. I waited to see if she was tricking me somehow, if she wanted to scare the shit out of me.

But she never came. Not all night. I couldn't sleep. And the next morning she didn't say anything. Not even when I said I was going to Mass.

I should use the pay phone to tell my mom I'll be late. But I don't feel like calling her, so I take out my journal where I keep my poems.

I gave a journal to Maria for her birthday last year. It was pink leather, with a string to close it with. But she didn't want to write poems. Instead she used it to keep track of all the things guys tell her. I've seen it. That's all it is. Page after page of that stuff. Can you believe it? She doesn't even write the guys' names. But she remembers who they all were. Like the one that says she's the hottest he's ever seen? That was Tom Perez at the fiesta this year. And the one that says damn girl, that dress gotta come off easy? That was Pedro, Fabi's date, at the Sadie Hawkins dance. Some guy at the gas station told her to look at those lips! Some don't even make sense, the way they're written down like that, with no explanation. She just writes what the guys say, word for word. Some are really cheesy. And some are just gross, like talking about her pussy, that kind of thing. She says they're gross, too, but she's laughing when she says it. None of them are really good. Like the kind of thing where you would say, oh my God, that's beautiful. I wish someone would say that to me.

She never writes it down when I tell her she looks adorable. Like when she puts all her hair in those skinny little braids. Or when she's reading for class, with her legs all tucked up. That's the perfect word for her. Adorable. I know because I've thought about it a lot, working on my poems. But she doesn't write down anything I tell her, ever. She'd rather write down all the stuff other people say, stuff they probably don't even mean. Like Dominic saying he loves me. He didn't even have to say that. But he did anyways. I asked Maria once why she wrote all that shit down. So she could remember silly she said, and she thunked my head with her huge-ass purple pen. Yeah right I thought. She never wrote down the bad things guys said. That she looks like a frog. That she wasn't all that. To stop bugging them.

I look through the pages of my journal. It's all about Maria. How I wonder what she's thinking. How much I miss her. What a loser! When I'm old and looking back at my memories, I don't want to think of what a loser I was. I wanna think I was cool. Yeah.

When Maria looks back, she's just going to remember that all the guys loved her. And she's not going to remember me.

I turn a new page and write about serving Communion today. I try to remember Father's sermon, that crazy jailed Vietnamese bishop, the woman sitting in front of me, what people's handshakes felt like. People lifting their hands, sticking out their tongues. Pete on the piano, and Gabe on the guitar. How after every Mass people are like chugging the leftover wine. How the chalices and stuff are so holy that you can't even wash them like normal. Every single thing I can think of, I write down. I even draw a cartoon of the purificator. I'm the purificator, he's yelling. It's the shit. When I've written it all down, I close the journal and just wait for Ms. Rowe to come out.

I've never done Adoration. I don't know, I guess Mom never told me to. Usually you just get Jesus at Communion. I guess Adoration's so that you can spend more time with Him, instead of swallowing the Body and Blood right away. Jesus is like in there, invisible. That's what they say. And you can just sit there and like stare at Him all you want, and no one will think you're weird cuz that's what you're supposed to do. In class, Ms. Rowe said it's not part of Him that's there, it's like all of Him. All at once. Coming down from heaven, over and over again and all over the world.

The first time I had Communion was in the second grade. I was seven. My mom's cousin had a video camera, and I watched the video later. I was sitting in the front pew because I was one of the shortest, in my white dress and veil, and I kept turning around to look to the back of the church. My relatives laughed at me, asking what I was doing, why wasn't I paying attention. I never told them that I'd seen my dad in the back, just for a second. But then he was gone, and I wanted to see him again. I don't know why. I couldn't wait until the end. We were lining up for Communion for the first time, and I was still looking for him.

I flip through my journal, but I can't look at it anymore. It's like I'm feeling sick just reading it. I think of going back inside, to do Adoration with Ms. Rowe. I would kneel on the cushion next to her. My hands folded, looking up. I would think about how things really aren't that bad. Mom being mad at me and me pretending not to know why. Dad leaving and me having all these feelings, the ones I'm afraid to tell people. I would think that it's not that bad, really. It's okay. I could even forgive Him for it, since He's there. And if He wanted, He could forgive me, since *I'm* there.

It doesn't mean that I do forgive Him, or that I will. It doesn't mean anything. I'm just thinking about it, is all.

To Visit the Cemetery

Olivia

It was hot and Olivia's feet hurt. Chenta was used to walking, to taking the bus or subway. That must have been why she was so much fitter. Short like Olivia, but leaner, tougher. Chenta's apartment was on a hill so steep, Olivia couldn't climb it without stopping to rest.

Chenta wore a straw hat, even though it wasn't summer anymore. Olivia wore brown sunglasses that yellowed the streets and buildings like an old movie. When she took them off, the color stuck to things, and she'd have to blink a lot to get the real color back. Even then, this wasn't a Mexico bearing the warm shades of pinks, yellows, and greens that somehow had come to represent the country in the States. Here it was mostly gray. But maybe it had always been that way.

Olivia was only six years old when her parents died, and she and Pandi and Orlando had gone to live in the States with Abuelita. Their brief visits back to Mexico were always timed around the picking up of a check. Their father had had a good job with the state, and after he died, the government paid Abuelita a certain amount for them each, up until they turned eighteen. They had to get it in person, so Abuelita would

89

bring Olivia and her brother and sister to see Chenta and Hector, their older siblings who had stayed in Mexico.

The reason for this visit was a wedding. Chenta's daughter, Claudia, was getting married, and Olivia had been asked to be the *madrina de lazo*. She had already purchased the string of beads she and the *padrino* would use to bind the newlyweds together, making a special trip to downtown Los Angeles. She'd bought a new dress, too. Moments after she had arrived at the family's small apartment, before Olivia had even had a chance to catch her breath after the four flights of stairs, Chenta had smashed the dress into the tiny, packed closet of the bedroom Olivia would share with her niece and Claudia's son, Pedro, assuring Olivia she would iron it before the ceremony. The dress was cream colored, with rose petals falling its length. Olivia had paid a little more than she had wanted, but it was hard to find nice dresses that she thought she looked good in these days. She'd gone to three different places before she'd found something she looked decent in, and she didn't have more time to look.

Knowing that Chenta was busy with preparations for the wedding, Olivia had suggested going to the cemetery on her own. But, unsurprisingly, Chenta had insisted on taking her. Jet-lagged and tired from running errands, Olivia wished *she* had insisted. Or snuck out the door while Chenta was on the phone. Or given her the slip on the bus. She could have set her own pace, had some time to think. Olivia wasn't afraid to be on her own in Mexico City. She knew how to get around, and her Spanish was perfectly adequate. But Chenta wouldn't have understood why she preferred to go by herself, and Olivia didn't feel like explaining. If she'd pushed the issue, she sensed that Chenta would have tried to persuade her not to go at all, and then they would have gotten into an argument.

"We're almost there," Chenta called over her shoulder. They were going to buy flowers for the grave, and Olivia struggled to keep up. Chenta and her husband owned a car, but they were not allowed to drive it on Fridays. In an attempt to limit the number of cars on the streets, the city blocked out a certain day for every vehicle. That's why they were walking.

They came to a lot. Vendors lined the far wall. There were open store fronts with tables set out in front, loaded with long-stemmed bouquets.

The stalls were numbered, one to ten. At the top of the building was a little niche just big enough for a small, colorless statue of Our Lady of Guadalupe. Mary was stuck in so many places in this country.

A *ramo* cost ten pesos, or you could get six for fifty. As soon as they entered, the vendors started calling to them, extending their bouquets so that Chenta and Olivia would pick their stall, their voices strong in the too-warm September air. "*Ven por acá. Mira, mira. ¡Qué bonitas! Rosas, señora. ¡Señora, rosas!*"

Chenta walked right up to someone and started bargaining.

"You should see this place on El Día de Los Muertos," she told Olivia. "They hike up the prices. So expensive."

Olivia's birthday was the day before El Día, on All Saints' Day. Since it was a holy day of obligation, she'd always had to go to Mass. It was something she didn't like, as she hadn't been very religious when she was young. Now with the new cathedral just opened up downtown, she planned to start a new birthday tradition out of going there for morning Mass, and then over to Olvera Street for lunch. Andi, always the architecture critic, had already questioned the cathedral's modern design. She was modern in every other way, so Olivia didn't understand what was so wrong with the cathedral. But even Andi would be impressed by the huge, bronze doors with all the different pictures of Mary. Olivia had read a story about them. It was supposed to be a building with no right angles. It made Olivia think of a paper lantern, or an accordion. Something crunching in on itself, or on the verge of either exploding or deflating. When she visited, Olivia would light a candle for Abuelita.

Abuelita had always said Olivia had a disposition for sainthood. She never said this when Olivia did anything good, but only when she was handing Olivia a mop or indicating the dirty dishes in the sink.

Chenta had already checked out a few tables and was now talking to a man in a blue baseball cap. "*How* much? What do I look like?"

Olivia looked at the flowers. Here were the colors she'd wanted. Reds and yellows and greens. But the tulips looked too fragile. The carnations, too ordinary. She wondered how many days it would be after she'd been back home in her quiet neighborhood of green lawns before all of these began to shrink.

A woman in the next stall was selling larger arrangements. Olivia admired one mostly made up of pink roses with one lily, one bird of paradise, and many small white flowers. Pink was not her favorite color. But at that moment it seemed like the only color that would do. "Those are nice," she said, seeking Chenta's approval. "What do you think?"

Chenta did not turn around to see the flowers. "Too much. You shouldn't pay that much for flowers."

Chenta went on haggling with the man.

It had been a hassle trying to get to pay for the dinner last night, too. They'd gone out to a restaurant at Plaza Garibaldi, where all the mariachis were. Chenta had grabbed the bill and made a big fuss, lamenting the family's decision to have ordered dessert. It had been a decision Olivia had encouraged, everyone ordering either flan or ice cream, except for Chenta who ordered nothing. Olivia had demanded the bill, but Chenta would not even let her look at it, and the restaurant was so crowded, she couldn't get up without making other people move. Eduardo, Chenta's husband, had taken Olivia's side, saying weakly, "If she wants," which did nothing to dissuade Chenta. It seemed like the rest of the family was thinking along the same lines, not saying anything, but hoping silently that Tía Olivia would be victorious in the battle for the check. That had made her feel bad for Chenta. But she had told her three times before they left the apartment that she wanted to treat them all to dinner. And wasn't that why she worked so hard? So she could spend her money the way she liked, without having to worry? She didn't want to be like Abuelita. Always calculating, always negotiating. The answer to everything, no. So many noes. She was all worn out by the end. Wasn't there more to life besides worry? And it wasn't every day she was in Mexico. Not every day she got to treat her family. Why did everything have to be so hard with her sister?

In the end, Chenta had extracted Eduardo's wallet, and Olivia had had to slip the money into Chenta's purse as they exited the restaurant, making a "shh" finger at little Pedro, who saw it all.

"I can get the flowers, Chenta," Olivia said. "We should be going. You've got to get back to the apartment."

But Chenta didn't seem to listen. "Don't throw your money away. Let me talk to them."

Olivia wanted to say she didn't care for the flowers Chenta was arguing over. That she wanted something special. She wanted to say she was tired. But that would make her sound like a little girl. And suddenly she felt like one, waiting for the permission of an adult to buy something. "Well, I'll just get these," she said aloud, though Chenta had her back to her, and she paid the woman for the big bouquet. When Chenta noticed what she had done, she shook her head at the man, and they stepped away from the vendors.

The bouquet lay in the crook of Olivia's arms, gorgeous, rebellious, shocking pink. She felt a little braver holding it. "Want to take a taxi?"

Vicenta

"Al Pantéon," Vicenta said to the driver and scooted back, feeling a prick in her shoulder where the vinyl must have been torn. She settled into the seat more, and then she didn't notice as much. Olivia did not sit fully back, her body visibly tightening when the taxi sped off, flying through narrow spaces between trucks and vans. Vicenta tried to get her attention, but Ollie did not look at her, just held the bouquet casually in her lap, keeping her focus out the window.

Vicenta turned her body to face her sister. "Is something wrong, Ollie?"

"No," she said, and Vicenta heard a trace of sadness.

Vicenta swiveled to face the front and didn't hide her heavy sigh. Ollie never wanted to talk about what was bothering her. "You have to be careful is all. People will try to cheat you."

She thought she saw a change in Ollie's eyes at this. Was it impatience she had glimpsed? Was Ollie thinking Vicenta was paranoid, or that she shouldn't care? Yes, that was it. Vicenta turned to look out her own window.

It was true she was concerned with spending. But who could blame her? Eduardo was still out of work, and she wasn't working two jobs, exhausted all the time, so they could throw the money away. There were the doctor bills from when the baby had gotten sick. And then there was the wedding. Claudia's wedding. She'd had to sit her only daughter down at the kitchen table and tell her sternly: She could not have flower arrangements. She could not have bridesmaids. She could not have a huge, beaded wedding dress. It had been hard, seeing Claudia's disappointment, her pouting. More than anything, her surprise. But how could she have expected anything different? Where was the money supposed to come from? How much had they spent on her *quinceañera*? Had Claudia forgotten about *that* big day? And for what? She'd gotten pregnant a year later, and now that she and her boyfriend were finally getting married, she wanted the fairytale wedding, too. A wedding Vicenta never had, nor would have dared to dream about. She felt a little guilty for thinking all this. But a big wedding was something Vicenta could not give her daughter, even if she wanted to.

Now that Vicenta was sitting in the taxi, she felt the pad between her legs scratching the inside of her thigh. She hoped it was holding up. There'd been some spotting this morning. Nothing big. But she felt so sweaty all over, it was hard to tell. On top of that, she'd forgotten to stick more pads in her purse, they'd left in such a hurry. Streaks of heat passed over her face, and she took a paper fan out of her purse.

Ollie ventured a look at her and her eyes softened. "The flashes?"

Vicenta nodded. She'd mentioned her symptoms when they were on the phone, arranging for Ollie's arrival at the airport. "It's all right."

Years ago, when Ollie had been eleven, she'd written to Vicenta, telling her she'd had her first period and what should she do. This had made Vicenta angry. Angry that her little sister was so far away. Angry that there was no one there for her to talk to. Not Abuelita, not Pandi, who was younger, no girls at school. What's more, the letter had been sitting in the *sala* for two days, and no one had told her about it. That night, she'd gone out and bought a calling card with the money she had saved from work and called Abuelita's house in Los Angeles. Ollie locked herself in the bathroom for privacy, and Vicenta shared all the stupid stories she'd heard when she was younger. Like that if you became a nun, God took away your period as a thank you. And you wouldn't be having kids anyways, so you didn't have to practice for the pain. They had laughed like crazy. And Vicenta had been able to stay on the phone. Not the two minutes she usually got when Tía let them talk.

No, she stayed on for a long time, until Abuelita told Ollie she had to get off already. That had felt good.

Vicenta still had the letter, though they hadn't spoken about it in years. She wanted Ollie to ask her more about her body's changes. She wanted to ask if Ollie had started experiencing her own. But the cemetery was coming into view. Now was not the time.

Olivia

Chenta handed the driver the fare through the window, which Olivia let her do since she had bought the flowers.

They had been spared some of the brightness of the day while in the taxi, but now Olivia had to put her sunglasses back on.

"It's so big," she said. "I'd forgotten."

Chenta's voice was flat. "Not big enough."

She and Chenta had talked about the situation during her last visit a few years ago, when their aunt had had to be cremated. The city had long since run out of places to bury its dead. For years, the policy had been that if one bought the land at the gravesite, one could bury another family member in the same spot after seven years. If one did not buy the land, as one was not required to, he gave up his right to it. If it was not purchased for *perpetuidad,* the grave would be dug up and used to bury someone else.

This cemetery was different from the one Abuelita was buried at in Rose Hills in Whittier, which was grassy and landscaped, dotted with well-manicured trees. Here, it was mostly cement, and many of the graves were covered with heaps of dirt and other debris. Dirt was everywhere, and not the growing kind. It was the kind you wanted to sweep up into a dustbin and throw away. There were still trees, but there used to be so many more. Like an orchard for as far as she could see, to the hills. Someone had left a Styrofoam cup with a pink straw sticking out on top of a grave. There was dark liquid inside, maybe Coca-Cola. A small PERPETUIDAD was etched onto a neighboring grave, looking like graffiti. Some crosses curved downward like they were bowing to her. Others looked as if they had been lying on the ground and were in the process of sitting up. These might have a statue on the tail. It was like the sculptor had wanted to make them seem alive, like they were one of those liquid metal creatures from a sci-fi movie her brother liked.

They couldn't find the grave at first, though they both agreed they were in the right general area. They could pay ten pesos at the front office to be told which was the exact site number, but Olivia didn't want to bring up this option.

"I thought you knew where it was," she said instead.

"I do, just give me a second. It's around here somewhere."

"When's the last time you came?"

"I don't remember."

Olivia didn't say anything. She walked by the graves, lingering to read the names. Most of the graves had little stone books at the top, carved to look as if they'd blown open to the middle. The names of the deceased were etched onto the stone pages.

She found one grave that was missing its book. Its big blue and white tiles, more reminiscent of a bathroom, looked familiar. This might be it. But where was the book? A panic seized her and her eyes darted to the surrounding area. There was a book lying on the neighboring grave, which was piled high with dirt and broken branches. Cocking her head, she read the names of their parents, "Aurora and Hector Real-Dominguez." The "Dominguez" was spelled "Dguez."

"Chenta!" she shouted. "This is it!" The shrillness of her own voice startled her. "The book must have been knocked off somehow," she said, more controlled.

Chenta came over. "Where?"

Olivia pointed. "But Chenta, how do we know?"

"That's it," Chenta said, nodding at the blue and white tiled one.

Olivia must have looked distressed because Chenta put her hand on her shoulder and repeated, "This is it, I am sure. See?" She stepped over Olivia and picked up the stone book, placing it on top of the grave, where it slid into place like a puzzle piece. "It fits."

"Yes," Olivia said and felt a little foolish for getting so upset.

Their mother had been the first to occupy the grave. Their father died just six months after. It was too soon, in more ways than one. He couldn't be buried with his wife immediately, so he was first left to a temporary rest in another cemetery.

Their birth and death dates were on the headstone. She had only a portrait to remember her parents by, and various photos collected over the years from relatives who would part with them. Of all the couple's children, she looked the most like their mother. She had the same almond-shaped eyes, gently sloping nose, and long lips. At night, sometimes, she'd run her hand over the landscape of her face to conjure memories that were far out of reach. If she had anything else in common with her mother, she didn't know it. Abuelita kept some pictures of her in the house, but she never spoke of her.

Her father was the casualty of a bus accident. Her mother died of cancer. Neither had seen a single grandchild. As Olivia looked down now, all she could think of was those pictures of them: handsome, young. Much younger than she was now.

She was pulling her rosary from a pocket in her purse when a young woman approached. She'd been standing a few yards away for awhile, not by any particular grave. Olivia wondered if she wanted to ask for money. The woman got close. "I can clean the stone for eighty pesos."

Vicenta

There were people in the cemetery who were not visiting anyone. They would approach visitors, offering to clean or restore a grave. Sometimes someone would pay them a large enough amount that they would maintain the grave each day, dusting and pouring water over it to keep it clean. That was how they made their living, or at least partly anyways.

This woman was young and nice looking. She wore a whitish T-shirt and sweatpants, which must have made her too warm in this heat. Her long dark hair was pulled back tightly into a braid. She moved in a comfortable, confident way. It was the same confidence Vicenta saw in women all over the city. The same she felt when she cleaned other people's homes, removing her shoes before stepping onto their carpet, wiping away all traces that she had been there. It was a confidence born out of necessity. Shame was a luxury they could not afford.

Well, a little still seeped in. Vicenta had not told Ollie about her second job. She would make too big a deal out of it. And she didn't want her to worry or offer money. Not like the last time. They'd already taken too much. She'd had to make Eduardo promise he would not say anything. Couldn't her sister come visit in peace? She'd even kept an extra eye on him, afraid he would try to approach Ollie when she wasn't around. He could tell, too. He knew what she was up to. He'd been quiet, restrained with her the past few days.

Once they'd given the woman clearance to work, she'd gone to get her other supplies. She had a broom. And she'd made a yoke out of a long, curved branch. A chain ran along it. She could attach two plastic buckets to it to carry water. The buckets had a wooden board turned sideways and fitted inside, a little metal ring drilled into it. Two letters were etched into the branch, S and M. "Santa Maria" was Vicenta's wild guess. She wasn't Catholic anymore, not since she married Eduardo, and she stopped going to Mass a while before that. Some people said if you were Catholic, you were Catholic for life. They were probably right.

Ollie was the one who had accepted the woman's offer to clean the grave, and that was fine with Vicenta if it made Ollie feel better. She'd been surprised at her own embarrassment over the condition of the grave. But why should she be embarrassed? She wasn't the only relative in the city. There were many others who could have visited. They still had aunts and uncles living. But she was the daughter, right? She was the Mexican daughter. As the young woman worked, it was too quiet, and Vicenta felt compelled to speak, to fill the air. "Our parents are buried here," she said to the woman. The woman smiled in reply.

"They died when we were just little. One aunt wanted custody and our grandmother disputed it. The judge decided to split us up. Ollie and our brother and sister went to live in the U.S., and I stayed here with our other brother."

Obviously Vicenta hadn't meant that they'd stayed in the cemetery. Still, she added, "In D. F."

When her sisters and brother had moved, Vicenta had imagined them camping out at the border, like her cousins had said they'd done, waiting for their chance to cross. She had felt bad for them, to be so uprooted. To have to leave their home and live with Abuelita, who was so old. But then, a few years later, news had come of their house. A real house with big yards in both the front and back. A washing machine and a garden and cars in the driveway. Her concerns suddenly felt foolish. When she was old enough, she saw the house for herself. She even tried to move to California. But the effort was halfhearted. It was already too late. She'd already begun seeing Eduardo, knew that he would be her husband one day. And it was more than that. It was *la ciudad.* When her younger brother went off to play with their male cousins, leaving her alone, the city had been there for her. When she couldn't go to school like she wanted and had to work to help pay the rent, it had been there. The city belonged to her. She knew at a young age that she would never leave it.

People came and just thought it was dirty and crowded and smoggy. And it was all those things. But Vicenta saw life in the streets, in the storefronts, in the amazing museums and the plazas and even churches. She didn't know why out of all the places to go, Ollie had to visit the cemetery. And especially when she was here for so short a time, and Claudia's wedding going on. Olivia was very religious, she knew. She believed in an afterlife. Why did she have to come here every single time she visited?

A tiny breeze stirred a stalk of stiff, colorless flowers standing on the neighboring grave. The woman continued working. How she could spend her entire day here, Vicenta didn't know.

Olivia

In no time at all, the grave was looking much better. The young woman poured the bucket of water over the blue and white tiles. Setting the bucket down, she wiped the excess water off with her hands. It spilled in little rivulets down the sides and pooled onto the ground. She smiled up at them, putting one hand on her knee and gracefully rising in one steady, fluid motion. "My husband," she said, and Olivia followed her gaze to a young man approaching.

"Is this your husband?" Chenta laughed. "Why aren't you working?" she called out to him. "You're just watching your wife clean away?"

It was obvious to all of them he was working. He carried a shovel, and his jeans were dirty up to the knees. Still, Olivia could tell he hadn't liked what Chenta had said. He smiled close-mouthed, humoring her. Olivia wondered why Chenta did not mind that people humored her. The young woman smiled good-naturedly at them both and placed her hand on his shoulder to welcome him into their circle.

"They are sisters," the woman said. "They look alike, don't they?"

The man got that certain look on his face, like men caught in a group of women will when posed with an uncomfortable question. But he looked sweetly at his pretty wife. He must have been a good husband. "Really? Which one of you is the oldest?"

"I am," Chenta said without hesitation, and Olivia felt a familiar twinge of uncertainty.

Growing up, Olivia had always claimed to be the oldest of her siblings. Explaining about her brother and sister in Mexico was usually more than she wanted to do. It sounded too complicated, too strange. And she had basically grown up as the oldest. Abuelita charged her with caring for Pandi and Orlando. She had to make sure they did their homework and ate well and got home at the proper time. But the role did not come naturally to her. She always felt unsure of herself, letting Pandi talk her way out of chores, Orlando running off whenever he felt like it. Maybe it was because of Chenta. Chenta, who was strong and no-nonsense. How could Olivia pretend, knowing she was out there?

The man removed his hat and politely addressed them, making it a point to look them in the eyes, like he had decided they would start from the beginning.

"If you want, I can put on another level."

"The book is off, too," Olivia told him.

"May I?" he asked. They nodded *sí, sí,* and he bent over and lifted the stone book, turning it over in his hands. "I could reattach it. It's not hard. I could fill in the letters, too. See how the paint has run out?"

Looking more closely, they could see that the words etched into the stone had once been filled with silver paint, most of which was gone.

"Seven hundred pesos. Then it will not get covered up like this again. You will be able to see it better."

Olivia could sense Chenta's hesitation. Her own nerves felt stretched, taut like the laundry line crossing Chenta's communal backyard.

"I'll do it for five hundred and fifty pesos if you decide right now."

"I don't think—" Olivia started.

"Do it," Chenta interrupted. She managed a smile. "If that's all right with you."

Olivia could tell that the smile was forced, but she accepted it. Chenta had given her an opportunity, and she produced the cash as quickly as she could.

"We'll pay you half now, and next Friday I will come to pay you the rest," Chenta told the man. He nodded and replaced his hat. It seemed fine to him.

"I'll go to my truck to get the supplies. I'll start when you are finished here. Take your time. I get more cement on Tuesday, so I will finish the job then."

Olivia and Chenta thanked him. His wife, who had been standing a few steps behind said, "Thank you. *Qué Dios te bendiga.*" She put her yoke on, and the man reattached the buckets without saying a word. He grabbed the broom, and they walked off.

When they were out of hearing, Olivia said, "I'm just going to pray for a bit, Chenta, and then we can go." The visit was taking longer than she had planned, and she felt bad about keeping Chenta out for so long.

Chenta just smiled. It was the smile that Olivia loved seeing on her. She looked calm for the first time this entire trip. "It's okay, Ollie. We aren't in a rush. It's nice and quiet here."

"Yes, it's nice."

Chenta let out a sigh and wiped her forehead with a handkerchief. "You don't have a maxi pad, do you?"

"Chenta!' Olivia scolded her. "Let's go to a store right now. I didn't know!"

Chenta laughed and shook her head. "It's okay. It can wait."

"But Chenta—"

"Ollie, if you argue with me anymore today, you'll have a grave of your own!"

Olivia sputtered at the thought, "If *I* argue with *you?*"

"Hey, get back here," Chenta said in English to the couple who was long gone. "I have a job for you. A grave for my crazy sister."

Olivia shrieked and swatted at her. "You're terrible." Chenta could have such a strange sense of humor. It still made her laugh though.

"Pray, Ollie," Chenta said, once they'd both calmed down. "You pray. I will arrange the flowers."

Olivia prayed holding one bead between her thumb and forefinger, the bottom loop of the rosary cupped in the palm of her other hand, the cross dropping lower and lower as she progressed. Olivia possessed a tangle of rosaries, gifts mostly. She'd bought this one herself at the mission in Santa Barbara, had it blessed by the priest after Mass. She liked the big, wooden beads, their sheen, the sound they made when hitting each other. There was a simple silver crucifix, and on the other end, in the middle of the third decade, a medal with Our Lady of Guadalupe on one side, El Santo Niño de Atocha on the other.

Years ago, the sisters at school had taught her how to pray it, how to ask Mary for her prayers and to remember the life and death of her Son. Olivia had learned it all—the different mysteries to meditate on, the appropriate days of the week for each, the longer prayers to say at the end. But in real life, her family had never prayed by the book. The Sign of the Cross may as well have been a countdown of "Ready, Set, Go!" because off Abuelita and her aunts and cousins would race, like horses around a track, sailing through the Our Father's and Hail Mary's and Glory Be's like if they stopped to do any more than take quick gulps of air, they'd lose their way, praying fast, fast, fast like that until they reached the end. So that was how Olivia prayed the rosary now, murmuring quickly in a monotone. She had always preferred praying in Spanish, even though it wasn't her primary language anymore. The words tumbled out, each one on the heels of the one that came before it, Chenta standing behind her, quiet. After a while, the words became just sounds, just breath moving past her lips. She saw Jesus on a hill and resurrected and bloody, her grown daughters as babies, Abuelita, before she died. By the time she got to the third decade—her fingers briefly squeezing the double-sided medal—all these images had faded away. And then it was just the words to get through.

She had brought the girls to Mexico, just once, for a Baptism many years ago. They'd gone to visit the cemetery, to see the grave of grandparents they'd never met. To La Villa, where Mary appeared to Juan Diego. For a gondola ride in the Xochimilco Gardens, each boat with its own pretty woman's name and a man paddling and rafts of whole mariachi bands floating by. To the castle of Chapultepec, where Maximilian lived with his empress. To the Pyramids of the Sun and the Moon in Teotihuacán. One surreal place after the next. Mexico must have seemed one great fairy tale to them. Even the cemetery, in a way. The sad part. Every fairy tale had its sad part.

Just like her and her sisters, Andi and Maura had wanted to peek into the mausoleums. To peer into the dusty windows with iron bars shaped into crosses. She and Pandi would speculate on whether the fruit and drink and flowers on the altars were real. Point at the statues of the Virgin and the faded *papel picado*. Sometimes the bottom chambers weren't even closed up right, and they could see underground, the slabs of concrete, empty, stacked like bunk beds.

At the last amen, the cemetery fell into silence. For just a few seconds, Olivia felt the quiet inside herself, like all words had been taken out of her.

She lowered the rosary back into her sweater pocket, where it coiled into a pile, and dabbed at her eyes with the hem of her sleeve. If Chenta could tell Olivia had been crying a little, she didn't let on. She offered Olivia her arm, and Olivia threaded hers through the crook, squeezing through the fleshy part of her sister's upper arm to the hard muscle underneath. Olivia bent to pick up her purse, and when she wobbled standing up, Chenta steadied her. The flowers they'd brought, in the white vase, looked like they were floating over the grave. They made one last Sign of the Cross, and went home.

What Would Mary Do: A Christmas Story

I

Dulce Moreno kneeled on the grass of her backyard, hugging her shoulders and shivering a little in the cold air.

The shrine had turned out quite well, Mary sheltered in a little house of brick that arched at the top, the lime and lemon trees on either side. It was an Our Lady of Grace statue—Mary standing, head bowed, with her hands lifted to the heavens and the snake underfoot. Luis had painted her skin a caramel color and her hair very dark brown. For her clothes, Dulce didn't want the typical Marian colors of blue and white. Luis helped her pick out a deep hunter green and a bright orange. He told her that her Mary was made of fiberglass and resin.

He'd even made a small base of blue and green tiles, with enough room for flowers and candles.

It had been working out so well between her and Luis. At least, that's what she had thought. Standing up, she wiped at the stains on her pants, barely caring that they were probably ruined. Her heels sank guiltily into the freshly planted grass, the grass that Luis would never set foot on again. Dulce picked a stray blade from Mary's robe, the beauty of the statue stinging her a little.

It had all started with the Virgin.

II

Dulce Moreno had never been worried about getting married. Well, not really. Yes, all her friends were married. And yes, she had attended her ten-year college reunion without pictures of babies, an engagement ring, or even a date. But there was still time for all that. Besides, her mother did enough worrying for the both of them. Dulce would wave her off when she pointed out the third potential husband of the day. They would laugh about it. But her mother always resumed. Dulce was thirty-five years old. If she wanted to know the joys of a family, there was precious time left. What about grandchildren? Fancy degrees and a career wouldn't keep her warm at night. And so forth and so forth.

The effect of this relentlessness was not a husband, but a very deep-seated, unshakeable faith. Dulce knew in her soul that despite whatever she did or wanted or thought, Mamá would win out in the end. As long as she was around to threaten making a profile on Match.com and randomly inviting older, well-situated men to dinner, everything would work out. But then Mamá passed away so unexpectedly, and everyone was saying they were sorry, bringing food, giving Dulce extra-long, rocking hugs. They were telling her she had to rest. She had to eat. She had to leave it all to God. No one was saying she should go out, buy new clothes, get a facial. No one offered to set her up with their cousin or neighbor or mailman. No one said anything when she put on ten pounds. When her mother left, there was an unquestioning acceptance. Dulce Moreno was fat and unmarried and getting old. And that was perfectly fine.

The thing was, Dulce had never seen herself that way. And neither had Mamá. She had hoped great things for her, a grand romance, a family.

Dulce spent the first few weeks after the funeral just getting by. Sitting on the couch. Packing up Mamá's things. She often regarded the Virgin. Mamá had won the statue at a raffle at the annual parish fiesta. She'd kept her on that small table that transformed into a sewing machine in the corner of the living room, donning her with a little crown she'd made from plastic grid, pearls, and gold thread. When her mother passed, Dulce inherited the house, along with most everything in it. Her brothers and sisters did not question this. Dulce had been the obedient one. When the others had run off with boyfriends or started opting out on the family tradition of Sunday Mass, Dulce had stayed.

Her mother had always talked about building a shrine for Mary in the backyard, but she'd never gotten around to it. Mamá was hardworking, but she also sometimes just liked to talk wistfully of things for years. She liked to have these little dreams, unfulfilled but within reach. Like Mary standing on the sewing machine, her palms out, waiting for Mamá to give her a proper home.

The Virgin was very heavy, though, as Dulce remembered from cleaning and confirmed again when she tried shifting her to change the cloth on the table. And Dulce didn't know the first thing about making a shrine. She was not a creative person. She had been told this countless times in school, at work, and by Mamá. The days passed, and it came to dawn on Dulce—this was not something she'd be able to do by herself.

Mary was of an in-between weight. Not big enough for a forklift. Not small enough for herself. Mamá, when she finally got around to it, would have asked one of the men on the block to help. Old men, still strong. Men who'd spent a lifetime working on their homes, their lawns, their cars. Dulce didn't want to ask them, though. They'd just want to ask about her mother, how Dulce was doing. And she didn't want to ask one of her sisters' husbands or her dopey brothers. After she hung up on the phone with them, they'd just say, "Poor Dulce, all alone in that house. How pathetic." All of her friends at the school were women, probably no stronger than she was. And asking one of the men at work did not seem professional.

In all her talk about finding a man, Mamá had always said to pick one who was handy. Yes, to "pick one," as if he were a cantaloupe at the market Dulce could lift out of the barrel and sniff. "He must be good with his hands!" Mamá would stress, as if it was the single determining factor between happiness and misery. "Don't make the same mistake I did. I married a bookworm. May he rest in peace." In the beginning, she would cross herself when saying this last part. But after so many recitations, the gesture lost its meaning. "What's a bookworm gonna do?" she'd rage on. "Read to the broken toilet? Do you know how many things break down in a house?" When her sons were seeming less than useful, she'd lament loudly, "For what do we have men in this house? ¡Pa' nada!"

The question of the Virgin began to obsess Dulce, occupying her mind when she cooked, even when she watched TV, the one activity that had always been a pleasant, mind-numbing distraction. All her life, she had always seemed to be running behind everyone else. While Dulce was still living with her parents, rushing home after a date to beat the sun, or parking in cars like a teenager, her contemporaries were moving in with boyfriends, getting married, getting pregnant either way, even getting divorced. Dulce knew she couldn't say it was virtue that had kept her from similar fates. It was due to stubbornness of a different sort that her life had played out the way it had. She had simply taken what had come, never reaching out of bounds for what had not. And now at the age of thirty-five, what did it say that she had no man in her life to ask to perform a simple household task? The more she thought about her current situation, the clearer it became. The brightness of her future had come down to this one defining moment. She could not borrow some man from another woman. It was very important that the man to move the Virgin be her own.

"Why don't you get a man from the corner? You could have him do other things, too," Elena told her one day. They were having coffee in the teachers' lounge, a dingy, unimaginative room, to be honest, but their only sanctuary from the students. Elena was the English and social studies teacher and her confidante.

"A man from the corner?" Dulce was surprised at the practical way Elena was approaching the problem, although she'd not confessed to her friend her bigger desire for a male companion.

"Yeah, you know by Tyler and Rush? By that brick place? They stand there in case someone buying bricks wants help building a wall. You know the place."

"I think so. The one with the statues and columns?" There was some kind of lot that held a bunch of concrete statues for gardens and landscaping. A sign overhead read, CONSTRUCTION PRODUCTS.

"That's it. I got one last month to help me finish repainting the house. Mike wouldn't help. You think it would kill him to get up a ladder. He's says he's too old. He's not too old to be playing Playstation at one o'clock in the morning."

"Elena," Dulce put a calming hand on her friend's arm.

"Sorry. You just go pick one up. They'll pretty much take anything you're willing to pay. It's easy."

Dulce considered. "What do I do with him afterward?"

"Afterward?"

"Yeah, when he's done. Do I drive him back to the corner?"

"You could." Elena seemed less sure of herself. "Or, he could just find his own way. You just ask him which he prefers. I think a lot have bicycles."

"Bicycles?" Dulce had only had a bike as a little girl. She had a vision of a grown man on her pink steed, with a white wicker basket and plastic streamers.

"Well, the one I got had a bicycle. Cuz it's cheaper, I guess. And they probably don't have licenses. *Pues, ¿quién sabe?*" Elena always asked her questions in Spanish.

"I don't know how I feel about letting a strange man into my house."

"Yeah, when's the last time you had any man at all in your house?" said Marisol. She'd breezed into the room, drained the coffee pot, set it back on the hot plate, and left just as quickly.

Dulce stiffened. She got up to turn off the coffeemaker. Marisol, the principal's receptionist, was not one of her favorite people. She shamelessly talked about her weekend exploits and put up photos of herself in the office wearing low-cut shirts.

"Ay, *qué sinvergüenza*," Elena muttered under her breath. "Don't listen to her, Dulce. Look, it's not a big deal. Everyone does it. *Mi abuelita* does it," she said and slapped her hands on the table as if that settled things.

"Yeah, but she's old. No one would want to, you know, try anything."

"Try anything? Oh! You're funny, *mujer!*"

Picking up a man turned out to be easier than Dulce thought. That is, once she'd gathered her courage. She drove by the aforementioned corner a few times. It took her three days to get up the nerve to pull over. When she did, she parked a little ways from where the men stood and kept the motor running so she could make a quick getaway if need be. But there was no commotion, no mob of men descending upon her screaming out promises of cheap labor. A single man approached the car. Dulce lowered the window, nervously glancing around the street to see if anyone was watching. Were there cops around? Could she get arrested for something like this?

"*Hola, Señora. ¿Necesita algo?*"

The man was young, in his mid-twenties probably. He had dark skin and curly dark hair. His smile was friendly, and she liked how he'd addressed her politely.

"Yes," she answered him in Spanish. "I need you to do some lifting. Nothing too big, but it's too big for me. I could help you. And then maybe some cleaning out of the garage, if it's not too much."

"*Señora,*" he said, "I'll do whatever you want. Moving furniture, painting, electrical work, plumbing, roofing, gardening. *Hago todo.*"

Dulce didn't know what to say to that. "Oh, okay." She opened the door, and the man got in. His seat was too far up. Smiling over at her, he slid the seat back, and buckled his seatbelt. Dulce turned to face the road. She had her man.

In the beginning it was awkward. They were both shy. Dulce afraid to ask for what she wanted, and Luis wanting to be gentlemanly. But they eventually settled into a very nice routine that seemed to satisfy them both. Luis spoke very little English, so they spoke to each other in Spanish. Dulce sometimes laughed over her *pocha* butchering, but Luis was always sweet about it and seemed grateful that he could speak his native language. For her part, Dulce felt happy hearing Spanish again in the house, like she was rediscovering new words. Familiar yet slightly different because Luis was from El Salvador, not Mexico. Her mother had spoken to her in Spanish, but she'd always answered in English. That was just their dynamic.

It was four months later when Dulce came back from work to find Luis picking oranges in the backyard. There was just time to make him some food before she dropped him off at the bus stop on Rosemead and Durfee, where he caught his bus to El Monte. He rented a back house in a small lot with a few other men. He always refused a ride home, though Dulce always offered.

She started preparing sandwiches and heating up some milk. She plopped the block of chocolate into the simmering pot of milk and smiled. The house was looking cheerful. Luis had put up the Christmas lights outside. He'd trimmed the shrubs and swept out the driveway. The garage was clean and clear. They'd together gone through all the old boxes and dressers, separating things into a junk and donation pile. She was feeling ready for Christmas.

Dulce pushed slabs of chocolate off the *tablilla* with her wooden spoon and stirred the milk, seeking out large deposits and mashing them up. When it was well mixed, she turned off the stove and poured the hot chocolate into a mug, took a pinch of cinnamon from the box and sprinkled it over the top. She grabbed a few sugar cookies from the cookie jar and set everything on a little tray she'd bought from Target once she started serving Luis lunch. Outside, one basket was already filled with oranges. Luis was looking at the statue of the Virgin. He made the Sign of the Cross and then turned to Dulce and smiled. She would brew coffee next time, make *café de olla*.

"*Hola, Señora.*"

He still called her Señora, after all this time.

"I made lunch," Dulce said, turning the tray a little to show him.

"*Gracias,*" he said quietly, and she set the tray on a chair. Luis dug into his pocket and took out something, holding it out for her.

"What's this?" she asked.

It was a key chain—a plastic heart with water and glitter inside, a little fabric rose in the center.

"They were selling them on the bus." Luis smiled and rubbed the back of his head.

"Oh, thank you, Luis. That's very sweet of you."

"I thought you'd like it. I noticed you don't have a key chain. Just that little ring for your keys."

"It was very thoughtful of you," she assured him.

Luis ran his hand through his hair again. "I'm really nervous." He laughed.

Dulce picked up an orange and sniffed it. "What about? These look ripe."

Luis bent down. Dulce wasn't sure why, maybe he'd dropped an orange.

"Ms. Moreno, there is something I would like to ask you."

"Oh?" Dulce said. She looked down and for the first time became alarmed.

Luis, this sweet young man from El Salvador who had been repairing her rain gutters and weeding her garden and watering her plants for the past four months had his hand over his heart. And somehow he'd taken one of hers. "I know we haven't known each other long."

The orange in Dulce's free hand landed with a soft thud on the freshly cut grass.

After dismissing Luis, in more than one way, Dulce returned to the kitchen and placed the untouched tray on the counter, then managed her way to a chair. What had she done? She hadn't meant for anything like this to happen. She hadn't flirted, hadn't encouraged something like this. She'd only wanted someone to help her with things around the house. Small improvements. Someone to share the time with, to give an opinion on how she'd decorated.

Dulce groaned and lowered her head onto the table. When she looked up, her eyes met the refrigerator. She was contemplating opening the Rocky Road ice cream she'd bought. A gallon, because she figured Luis would have some.

There, taped over the door of the freezer was the Posadas schedule she'd cut out of the church bulletin. They'd already started on the sixteenth. Two cheap computer graphics were located in the lower corners, one of Mary being led on a donkey by Joseph and another of two modern faces smiling over the crib of Jesus. Normally, activities for the two language groups were separated, but in this schedule they were listed together. *Pescador de Hombres*. Altar Servers and Knights of Columbus. *Pequeñas Comunidades*. Mamá had been a member of a pequeña comunidad, a prayer group that met once weekly. She'd been very active in the Spanish-speaking community at the church. Immediately after her death, Dulce had avoided the members. Not because she disliked them. Her connection to them had been through her mother, and talking to them without Mamá there had seemed like too much at the time. But thinking of them now, she felt something like homesick.

Mamá used to make a big thing of Las Posadas, packing extra sweaters, water, snacks, a flashlight. It was as if they were hiking up into the mountains and not just walking the streets of South El Monte for half an hour. Dulce's father had never gone, and her brothers and sisters had grown out of the tradition, preferring to watch the Christmas specials on television. But Dulce had accompanied her mother every year for as far back as she could remember. It was her favorite thing about Christmas. She could make them tonight, if she hurried.

III

Dulce Moreno had not taken two steps before she was intercepted by Sister Martha Frances in the church parking lot. The Benedictine nun had a garment draped over one arm, her blue eyes very bright. "Our Mary ditched us for an open bar. You don't mind, do you?"

"But, Sister, I was hoping I could just—"

"I knew I could count on you, Dulce."

Sister leapt at her, and Dulce stifled a yelp as she suffered a brusque makeover at Sister's hands. Sister yanked the pins out of Dulce's standard bun, letting loose the long, curly hair she never knew what else to do with, and pocketed her glasses.

"I'll need my glasses to see the lyrics, won't I?" Dulce asked, making a weak motion toward Sister's pocket.

"You'll manage," Sister said.

Apparently, her glasses were inappropriate attire. Nose rings must have been also, which must have ruled out the teenage girls Dulce saw when she joined the rest of the group in the cafeteria. They never gave the role to a teenager, even though that would have been more historically accurate. Between the teenagers and middle-aged women, she had been deemed the most appropriate woman for the role.

They started in the cafeteria with a rosary. As usual, Dulce had to master the miracle of suspended breathing to keep up with the rushed Spanish prayers. Then they'd begun their journey with a walk through the parking lot, wet from an earlier drizzle, to the preselected houses across the street. Dulce's high heels clicked noisily on the pavement. The black pumps were mostly covered by the robe, but she still felt self-conscious, as though there were something inherently indecent about being Mary in high heels, like crossing one's legs during Mass.

It was an unusually cold December. The angels flanking her, two boys and two girls, wore sweatpants and long sleeves underneath their white robes. Dulce recognized them as second-grade students from the school.

The porch light at the second house on the route wasn't working. The man playing Joseph illuminated the sheet music by holding a small flashlight over the page they shared. Dulce did her best to block out his off-tempo singing as she leaned in to read the lyrics. Luckily, the small crowd of people behind them knew what they were doing. The melody of the song was easy enough to pick up, even to those unfamiliar with it, but she always forgot the words.

After the third house, they circled back to the church grounds to finish with the piñata and treats in the Covered Area. Only once in a blue moon did Dulce remember what a funny name that was. She had been calling it the Covered Area since she went to elementary school there herself. It was cleared of most of the benches where the students took their lunches. A life-size nativity scene was set up at one end, and on the other a long counter was lined with cups steaming with *champurrado* and coffee and plastic bags filled with *pan dulce*. The star-shaped piñata hung from a rafter in the middle of the building.

The group sang a few more verses by the nativity scene, marking the conclusion of Las Posadas. Joseph gave her a hug, and the women grasped her hands and kissed her cheek. She didn't see Sister anywhere, but then, the old nun had taken her glasses. Dulce made her way over to the food, squinting, but not before removing the Mary costume.

There was a long line of children at the piñata now. The hitting had started. The crowd was singing, "*Dale, dale, dale,*" in encouragement to a little girl with the bat. A few of the children waved at her. She smiled and waved back.

Dulce got a drink and pan dulce and settled at a table. She hadn't had the reflection time she'd been seeking when she made the decision to attend and was hoping to sit for a while undisturbed, not wanting to return home just yet. She was testing the heat of the champurrado with her finger when Sister appeared.

"Thank you for pitching in, Dulce."

"You're welcome," Dulce answered distractedly, sucking her finger.

"Do you want me to take that back?" Sister held out her hand for the robe.

"I'll wash it for you, Sister. I'm doing laundry tomorrow."

"You're too good, Dulce. Oh, don't forget these." Sister fished the glasses out of the pocket of her sweater and set them on the table.

Dulce smiled, reaching for them and slowly wiping them with the hem of her shirt.

"You know, Dulce, you really remind me of your mother. She said yes to everything. Fundraisers. School trips. Everything we needed help with."

"She was incredibly giving." Dulce was happy to hear Mamá was appreciated.

"Yes. And she loved you very much."

Dulce smiled.

"I think she needed you too much, but it's hard when you're alone." She gestured to herself. "Growing older."

Dulce was going to ask what she meant, but Sister went on speaking.

"Delight in the Lord, and He shall give you the desires of your heart."

"Yes, Sister." And then because Sister seemed to want more of her, Dulce said. "I know, I need to pray more."

"Prayer is good. But God isn't the only one to talk to." Sister looked out the open space toward the small parking lot. "Don't forget that there are people nearby. People God puts in your path. Opportunities."

"You mean, taking up another ministry?" Dulce had been slacking. Sister had probably noticed.

"You might want to check out the Christmas boutique, Dulce," Sister said, her voice becoming stern. "They've got some nice things for sale. And Santa's taking orders. Remember what I said."

Dulce nodded, though she wasn't sure which part of the disconnected speech Sister was referring to and didn't want to ask her to clarify. She envied her her certainty, her vocation. "Sister, how did you know that you were being called? I mean, was it really obvious or only—"

"Good-bye, Dulce."

Dulce walked toward her car, the robe bunched in one hand. She had her keys out and tossed the robe inside. It deflated upon contact with the passenger seat. Dulce paused, staring at the robe. What was it after all but just a cloth? The color of those medical gowns in the hospital. What did it mean anyway? She thought of going home to the quiet, to the baskets of oranges Luis had piled up. She closed the door, locked the car with a beeping sound, and walked back to the conference room where the Christmas boutique was being held. The click-clack of her high heels sounded normal again.

It was warm inside. Some of the tables had packed up, but business was still being done.

Someone came up behind her. "Ho, ho, ho!"

Dulce turned, ready to smile politely at the elderly man they usually got to play Santa. But she was surprised. "Robert, is that you?"

Robert Lara was the music teacher at the school. He wasn't full-time. Dulce, who kept the books as a second job, knew they couldn't afford it. But twice a week, Mr. Lara would give her class a music lesson, and afterwards, she would always have a time trying to get them to settle down, to ready themselves for the rigors of math.

Robert shrugged, pulling back his beard so she could see his face and whispering confidentially, "The regular Santa bailed."

"Let me guess. Open bar?"

"How did you know?" He grinned and adjusted his hat. His eyes seemed bigger and warmer than she'd noticed in their few previous encounters.

"Your hair's down," he said.

"Thanks." She answered. "I was at Las Posadas," she said quickly, realizing he had not actually complimented her hair. His eyes had a look of admiration in them though.

"Las Posadas. And how did they end?"

"Well, we came into . . ."

"Dulce, I was kidding."

"Oh." She got it. She was not doing too well in this conversation. She knew there was a reason she was still single.

"Dulce, can I ask you a personal question?"

"Of course." She kept the smile on her face, although she dreaded what was to come. He was going to ask what he should get his girlfriend for Christmas, or something similar in nature. She was always getting those types of questions from men.

"It's really personal," he warned her.

"It's okay." But it really wasn't.

"When is the last time you sat on Santa's knee?"

"Excuse me?"

"Santa's knee. When's the last time?"

"I'm not sure . . ."

He turned around, and she thought he'd finally given up on her. But he sat on his special Santa chair and lifted his hands, presenting his knee. Or really, his lap.

"Robert." She came closer, just so she wouldn't have to raise her voice.

"Hey, this is what I'm here for. I said I'd be Santa, and I'm going to be Santa. I make a good Santa, don't I?" He patted his stomach. "¿Sí o no?"

"Sí." A funny memory crept up. "Except—"

"What?" A comical look of panic struck him. "Tell me, please. I want to be the best Santa I can be."

"It's just that—"

"Yes?"

"The Santa *I* knew," she said, bringing him to smile, "*He* spoke with a heavy Spanish accent."

"*Ay, sí, mija. ¿Cómo no?* I was jus' gonna tell d'you, I come from my workshop in Chihuahua. All right, leetle girl. D'you know what d'you like for the Christmas holiday?"

Dulce couldn't contain the laugh that popped out of her mouth. She bit on her nail and glanced around the room.

There were students present. And there was Marisol, lurking with her camera, probably salivating for more material to gossip about. But, for once, Dulce didn't care about what Marisol did or saw.

She got a little closer, and then a little closer, till she was standing right over Robert. Placing a hand on his shoulder, she lowered herself onto his lap, gently. He felt solid beneath her, and she slowly relaxed, allowing him to bear her full weight. His hand went to her waist in a gesture of support. His face was very close. Dulce shut her eyes tight like she used to when wishing on stars, leaned in to his ear, and proceeded to say with great detail what she wanted. Not just for Christmas, but for every day in her life. Things she wanted, but also things she wanted to be, for someone. These were things she'd been too afraid to tell even Mamá. Not because she wouldn't understand. But because then maybe Dulce would have to do something about it. Something that would involve stepping out of where Mamá could protect her.

Dulce finished her wish list and pulled away from Robert's ear. There were flashes going off and Dulce was momentarily blinded. When the bright spots receded, she could see Santa, blushing.

ACKNOWLEDGMENTS

I am immensely grateful to those over the years who have read these stories in some form, including Susan Compo, Jessica Krueger, Adrienne Rosado, Michael Sarabia, Erasmo Guerra, and Don Weiese. Thanks to Roberto Márquez, who selected my collection as the winner of the Miguel Mármol Prize. Thanks to Northwestern University Press, for publishing this work with such energy and thoughtfulness, and special thanks to Sandy Taylor, whose legacy lives on in the books and voices he published at Curbstone Press.

This work has found inspiration and support in many people. I am fortunate to be a part of the Macondo Foundation, which fosters a community of extremely talented and generous writers. Much love to my friends in South El Monte and El Monte, for just being themselves and having me around; to my sweetheart, for being the voice of both reason and comfort; to my family, for their enthusiasm; to my father, who shared his love of reading with me and my sisters; and most of all to my mother—I could not have done this without you.